the **americas**

also in **the americas** series

Breathing, In Dust by Tim Z. Hernandez
The Centaur in the Garden by Moacyr Scliar
Changó, the Biggest Badass by Manuel Zapata Olivella
Daughter of Silence by Manuela Fingueret
The Fish Child by Lucía Puenzo
Hut of Fallen Persimmons by Adriana Lisboa
Kafka's Leopards by Moacyr Scliar
The Last Reader by David Toscana
Mariposa's Song by Peter LaSalle
The Neighborhood by Gonçalo M. Tavares
The Origin of Species and Other Poems by Ernesto Cardenal
A Stitch in Air by Lori Marie Carlson
Symphony in White by Adriana Lisboa
The War in Bom Fim by Moacyr Scliar
Timote by José Pablo Feinmann
Unlucky Lucky Tales by Daniel Grandbois

A Taste of Eternity

A Taste of Eternity

a novel

Gisèle Pineau

translated by C. Dickson

Texas Tech University Press

This book is typeset in Fairfield. The paper used in this book meets the minimum requirements of ANSI/NISO Z39.48-1992 (R1997). ♾

Designed by Ashley Beck
Cover design by Ashley Beck

Library of Congress Cataloging-in-Publication Data
Pineau, Gisèle, author.
[L'âme prêtée aux oiseaux. English]
A taste of eternity : a novel / Gisèle Pineau ; translated by C. Dickson.
pages cm. — (The Americas Series)
ISBN 978-0-89672-870-7 (paperback) — ISBN 978-0-89672-871-4 (e-book)
I. Dickson, C., translator. II. Title.
PQ3949.2.P573A6413 2014
843'.914—dc23 2014003527

14 15 16 17 18 19 20 21 22 / 9 8 7 6 5 4 3 2 1

Texas Tech University Press
Box 41037 | Lubbock, Texas 79409-1037 USA
800.832.4042 | ttup@ttu.edu | www.ttupress.org

A Taste of Eternity

1

For she who sings
at the crossing of the ways

Lila—her life had been like a small vial that she'd been clutching awkwardly in both hands for a long time. As if she hadn't known what to do with it, until she began to shake it up. At first just to see the yellow sands settled at the bottom ripple and churn. See the sudden swelling of white waves, delicate lacy walls. Wait for them to come crashing down one after the other following a rain of yellow stars.

Yellow cotton stars hanging in the black sky.

So then she invented a blue horizon, like a theater prop, that she herself had splashed with gouache and then evened out with the nipple of her breast, the tip of her tongue, just out of curiosity, to familiarize herself with the softness, the salty taste of that sky before taking flight.

She often put her eye up to the vial. She saw people there who no longer existed, but whose reflections sent the sound of voices echoing out over and over. Ghostly laughter and crying and screaming. Grave faces from the past asking her to join them popped up at times and then gradually faded away, as earthly lovers do.

One day, the vial slipped between her fingers and shattered into a thousand pieces, releasing the troubled and furious waters of her life.

2

It was the month of December 1993, just before Christmas.

Lila's funeral.

Hands gripped shovels and threw earth onto her wooden coffin.

Lila, my old white mama, who had confided the underside of her life to me and then left me here alone. Everything she had been was crowding into my mind that day, a bunch of disparate memories in which the essential and the extraneous intermingled. Incredible love-dances that sent arms and legs flying, uplifted the soul, and turned time around.

Lila, how I loved her laughter.

And I'd never grown tired of the wonderful stories she told, tales and lies overlapping, faded truths . . .

"Ha! Ha! Ha! If you only knew, Billy! What a circus it was back in the days of the black market in Paris! If you knew what I went through, Lord! Don't pay any attention to my wrinkled up skin, my flabby thighs, and my crazy days. I knew a lot of men in my time. . . . Some of them used to get down on their knees before me and lick me all over, and all I had to do was spread my legs and snap my fingers, Lucien, Marcel, and Ferdinand and others who came from so far away, set down upon my path by chance."

And I loved it when Marcello's laughter joined in with hers, my son Marcello . . .

It was cold. My fingers were freezing despite the leather gloves. Black gloves that Lila had given me not long after I arrived in France. In those days, her closets and drawers, like her mind, were filled with memories. You'd have thought that all she'd ever done was pile up bits and pieces of her life. Never found anything to throw away or lend to anyone before Marcello and I came into her life. At first glance, it all looked like a bunch of innocent souvenirs, just for the sake of appearances, and it didn't even smell like mothballs. A well-conserved, living, vibrant past that was so exciting it made you want to go back in time in spite of the war. In those moments of confidence, Lila's tales were lighthearted, told only halfway, simply to impress us, invent parts of her life, make us laugh and cry. For years, she had left the things that really mattered to her—that frightened or wounded her as soon as she thought of them—in dark corners or secret drawers of her dressers. And so to cheer herself up, she'd pull out mountains of old clothes: collections of sequined silk or velvet evening gowns, flannel suits, jazzy shirts, men's pleated trousers, real fur coats. And boxes of hats, with wide brims, feathers, and veils, berets, pillboxes. Shoes of every color and all periods, crepe, spike, or wedge heels, patent leather pumps, with rounded or pointed toes. Crocodile skin pocketbooks, rhinestone clutch bags, beaded purses . . . When Lila had finished emptying out her closets, had learned to know me, she began to break free from the darkness that terrorized her.

On some mornings, she would wake up electrified, her eyes still stitched up with the black threads of some bad dream. She would call up the stairwell: "Billy, Billy! Come down!" And I'd barely stepped through her door when she'd hand me a wad of paper money pulled out of her brassiere, wrinkled, warm, ochre-colored five-hundred franc notes. . . . "Take it, and don't try to refuse, Billy! It's for you! For you and Marcello. You know I have no family! And we have to leave him a nice little pile! I don't want him to be in need later." And she'd start laughing. If I resisted, her blue eyes would turn into two hard stones, like those set in the rings on a princess's finger. I wasn't asking for anything. There was no reason that she should deprive herself for us. I had my job as a nurse at La Salpêtrière; it was enough. I would push her away. But I always ran up against the hard bones of her hands. Once she'd stuffed the bills into my pockets, she'd declare: "Billy, you know perfectly well that you're all I have left! Silly how one gets attached, even to black people!" Then she'd repeat herself until her tongue got too heavy and could no longer pronounce the word *black*. Until her jaw got a cramp in it. Until her eyes started watering.

Lila had been married only once in her life, in 1952, to Frédéric Montrevault. They'd lived for three years in a private hotel in the eighth arrondissement. He was a successful businessman. He kept his profits in the bank vault and owned several buildings in Lyons and Paris. When he died, Lila inherited a fortune and came back to her cherished apartment on rue Danton where she had once simply been one of Frédéric's tenants. Then she began piling up the bits of her life. Her phantoms and her lovers.

"There were gossips that said I only married him for his money. But you've got to believe me, Billy! We loved each other as much as we could. He was so kind, you can't imagine. Back then I was twenty-eight, and he was over sixty-seven. But we married for love, Sybille. And I hope you'll believe that! Don't go acting like those people who screwed up their mouths and sniggered when they looked at him. I loved my Frédo! I was his last ray of sunshine . . ."

The men who were digging Lila's grave had red noses because of the cold, and their shoes were ridiculous. They were wearing worn striped T-shirts under their sagging plaid jackets. You'd have thought they were clowns.

Their hands were tending to Lila's old body for the very last time. And I imagined her, stretched out ice-cold in her box, between the white satin and the purple lace, playing her last role, listening to the shovels of earth thudding in rhythm on the coffin, and smiling as if it were all just a farce. Smiling because she was reading my thoughts. She could see that grief wasn't keeping me from dreaming of the birds at The Kreyol and of packing my bags.

Two clowns wearing baseball caps backwards who were spying on one another with cigarette stubs in their mouths, stealing furtive glances at each other with the worried look of someone who's about to have a cream pie thrown in his face or a bucket of water dumped on his head.

I'd been curious about those two from the beginning. Intrigued by them and their red noses, their square hands with dirty, broken nails—they'd never known Lila. They seemed to have escaped from some circus, like lions, tigers, and panthers sometimes do. They were only there to bury Lila, turn death into a joke.

I wasn't crying. I was standing very straight in front of the grave, stiff with cold and feeling as if I were being orphaned a second time. Alone with my thoughts, the clowns, and Father Michel, who was reciting his prayers. Nice warm words, whispered into the icy wind that formed white plumes, evanescent angels come down to take Lila away.

I felt immaterial myself.

The world had tipped into irreality. The loose earth was flying up in slow motion. The movements of the gravediggers reminded me of a piece of choreography I'd found entertaining one day on television. I saw Lila smiling in her coffin. Smiling at the thousands of birds perched all around on the black branches of the trees. Stripped of their leaves, they seemed to be charred, still standing, but already dead, resuscitated from the days of the bombings that Lila would sometimes call up from her memory.

"You'd have been scared to death had you lived through that, Billy! Paris was no longer Paris! We never knew whether we'd be crippled or arrested or killed before the end of the day! We were hungry, we were frightened. Love was the only thing that enabled us to believe in life . . . and to eat too, Billy . . . You had to eat every day, you can understand that! Love was the only way! I was a naked dancer. I put my body up for sale to buy my topinambours, to buy rutabaga, roasted malt, margarine, and lard. . . . I plied fifty different trades while the people where you come from were belly-dancing bare-breasted under the coconut trees. I held all kinds of odd jobs, Billy! Waitress at the Jacquot Club, seamstress and salesgirl for expensive lingerie at Messaline Dedray, chambermaid at the Hotel Sextus on rue Alfred-Chicot, usherette at the Midi Theater, and also actress, yes ma'am!"

Instead of praying and asking the Lord to take good care of Lila, I was locked into horrible, comical, and fantastic thoughts. Thoughts like perhaps the devil lived in that cemetery and would soon come to take Lila away because she hadn't been a model of saintliness, had had a blast rolling her ass around in too many beds, loved too many men . . . Like surely the dead would rise up any minute from their graves and grab me too because I wasn't crying. Like maybe the birds sitting in the branches of the trees were Lila's past lovers.

My heels were sinking into the snow, and I felt as if I were being pulled backward. And I might well have fallen flat on my back, frozen stiff, just like an old tree, if I hadn't felt Father Michel's gaze upon me. Then I signed myself and threw my red rose into the grave.

At times, it was always just before midnight, Lila would begin to philosophize. I didn't like it when she forced me to dine on her theories. She started talking louder and louder and pouring herself huge glasses of whiskey while puffing on Chesterfields. No matter how I tried to order her with my eyes to keep quiet because Marcello was sleeping, and especially to loosen her fingers from around poor Johnny Walker's neck, she would get herself all fired up and advise me not to let people tell me what to do and run me into the ground. "You've got to enjoy yourself, Billy! You've only got one life, and it belongs to you! Don't lose a crumb of it, Billy! I'm not trying to push you into latching on to just anything . . . I'm not advising you to not give anything to others like those rich slobs that won't give up a penny. Billy, I used to do everything with grandeur and panache! I loved men without restraint and without too much regret. Fear, Billy, you can't imagine how poisonous it can be. Grandeur and panache—pointless words, you'll probably say, but they lend a sparkle to one's memories. And when love comes your way, make the most of it. Nothing in the world can beat it . . ."

In fact, I had the feeling she was going off on a tangent in her little philosophical talk, to avoid bringing up the fragile and sharp things she kept closed up inside, in little vials, small porcelain and crystal vessels sitting on one of the tables of her memory, that she avoided looking at, for fear of awakening their contents.

People had known and loved her in the past. Men especially, because women hated her. Lila was one of those dazzling people who cast a shadow on everyone else as soon as they alight anywhere. Very aged and tarnished, she still held a bit of that light, a light which was at once chilling and bright. She told me about the old days when she was trying to become a thespian and a singer in the midst of the war and how she'd almost become a new Michèle Morgan . . .

"But I loved life too much, Billy! And not discipline . . . You should have seen those poor girls, fresh from their hometowns, hanging around in voice classes backstage at the theaters. In the daytime they worked like slaves for dressmakers or factories. And evenings, they gave each other cues, rehearsed until they were exhausted, and dreamed. They had faith, Billy! They imagined they would act next to the greatest stars, throw their heads back and receive Gabin's kisses. Some of them were real bitches and double-crossed each other just to land a lousy part as a maid at the Théâtre de la Madeleine, and they waited around for hours at the stage door to slip a note to Guitry. Sacha wrote roles just for me, now that impresses you, eh?"

Sometimes, just for Marcello, Lila would drape herself in curtains or she'd take out her old silk dresses. She'd sing Mistinguett songs, recite whole monologues from plays. Sitting deep in Lila's red velvet armchair, Marcello was delighted. It's true that her makeup was outrageous. Lipstick too red that ran over the edges of her very thin lips, black pencil marks in the place of eyebrows that she'd shaved all her life, and her skin that looked like curdled milk covered with pink powder. Gobs of powder so that whenever she passed her reflection in a mirror she could feel as if she were still young and would remain so forever.

Soldiers, captains, lords and lordlings, and lowdown double-crossers had let their hands roam over her, turned her this way and that, hugged and caressed her. She'd loved them all, in her own way, with her heart, with her body.

Not one of them was there on December 15, 1993. Not even Henry who didn't want to see her in death. So I alone represented the family and friends of Lila's entire lifetime. And to console myself, I imagined two or three invisible beings praying beside me.

"May you rest in peace in your final abode, Elisabeth Louise Montrevault," Father Michel was saying as he set his wire-rimmed glasses straight. Together we made one last sign of the cross, and then he dusted off the snow that had stuck to his cape. A long black magician's cape. The clowns were gathering up their shovels in a wheelbarrow. For a second, I thought that Father Michel might take out a magic wand from his cape and resuscitate Lila like in the circus numbers when the girls are cut in two in a box and then jump up whole again, night after night, always to a new, spellbound audience.

Night after night, for nearly seventeen years—Marcello's age today—I dropped in to see Lila, listened to her old sentimental stories, looked for the phantoms that she saw wandering on the roof of the building facing us. Before going up to my place on the third floor, I would stop in on the second.

"Your little Lolo's got two mamas, doesn't he, Billy? And I know him better than you do! Marcello's my son! The two of you are all I've got in the world, eh, Billy?"

When he was a baby, she'd keep him at her place all day long. They loved each other. And the year I went to live in Noisy, with

Patrick, they phoned each other every day. Lila refused to believe that I'd moved away for good, that I'd taken her Lolo away.

"You come back whenever you want to, eh, Billy? I won't rent the apartment. If things don't go right with Patrick, if he's mean to Lolo, just forget it and come on home! Promise me . . . for sure? And don't forget to call me!"

I was back after nine months. She said, "Don't let it get you down! There's a man out there waiting for you somewhere. You'll find him all right. A man made just for you . . . Give him a chance!"

Sometimes the light that shone in her eyes would blink out all of a sudden. She'd sit hunched down in her red velvet armchair, utterly still, silent. That's when the bad memories that were crowding up inside her would suddenly come to the surface, monstrous tentacles gagging and pinning her down. She would just sit there, prostrate, for days on end. Didn't laugh. Didn't cry. Petrified, she counted and recounted the stars, the vials, the crystal and porcelain vessels that clinked against one another till they broke in her mind and wounded her heart. When he was very small, Marcello thought she was playing dead. He tried to awaken her, climbed up on her lap, pulled the three perennial hairs that grew on her chin. Lila wouldn't budge. Her blue eyes were seeing things from another time, people on the roof of the building facing ours, black and white children amidst the pigeons of Paris, scenes from a theater where she'd played, where she'd had a role that had marked her for life. But it was especially the war years that tormented her.

After two or three days, she'd be back among us, exhausted, as if she'd been severely beaten. And there was terror in her eyes, sparks of fear more deeply lodged in her than a long-term illness. At times like that, she couldn't stand for us to drag our feet or let a chair fall overhead. Marcello and I would put on our slippers and pad about as quietly as cats. Other times, it was the contrary—the silence made her temper flare. Crazed, she would knock hard on the ceiling with an old theater staff . . . "Are you all dead up there? I don't hear a thing! Anyone home? Heyo, you laid-low Negroes!"

When she came back to her senses, she'd beg Marcello to repeat the cruel words she'd shouted at us. She'd avoid me and start weeping into knotted up dishtowels or worn sweaters or old stockings, letting out little squeaks like a mouse. She'd swear she was so furious at herself she could slit her veins, swallow pills, and spit on herself. She'd assure us that she just couldn't understand why she'd called us *Negroes* because she liked black people. To prove it, from one of her albums—always the same one, with dog-eared corners—she'd pull out a picture showing a smiling black man with a soldier's cap on his head. On the back was written: "1945, Henry, forever . . ." *Faut rêver* (gotta dream), read Marcello. Lila shook her head and corrected him: "It's English, pronounce it *forévère*, it means *always* . . ." And inspired, she'd go on and force us to decipher and admire stacks of *Merry Christmas* and *Happy New Year* cards that handsome Henry, a New Yorker by adoption, had been writing her for nearly fifty years. She'd kiss the picture of Henry, ask our forgiveness a thousand times over, allow us to scrutinize the face in the picture a little longer before carefully putting her relics away. Then she'd disappear into her kitchen and beat egg whites for ages to make a cake of contrition that she'd force us to eat while she sat there wringing her hands.

Henry met Lila on the day after the Liberation of Paris. Originally from Saint John, he was one of those English-speaking West Indians living in Guadeloupe, who, having joined the dissident groups, braved the patrol ships from *La Jeanne* to respond to General de Gaulle's call to join the Free France movement and discover Europe. When he arrived in Paris, the day after liberation, people already mistook Henry for an American, with his English accent, his easy ways, and his love of chewing gum. At the time, Lila had given up waiting for news of Hans, her wartime sweetheart.

They loved each other for one whole year. But when neither Paris nor Lila wanted anything more to do with him, it was only natural that Henry chose exile in America to build a new life for himself. He'd seen too many countries, too many cadavers too, and he refused to consider the idea of burying himself alive on his island, at Hamilton's Gardens, where his mother Jenny had worked in the kitchen for years and years. America was a long way away. A long way from the Eiffel Tower and the Arch of Triumph that he held in childish admiration. A long way from the Porte-Bonheur, where Lila sat on his lap for the first time. A long way from her soft warm bed. A long way from regrets and the echo of all the forevers he'd whispered into the small of her back, between her breasts. America! With a dollar you could bet on a lucky star and dream up a fortune.

I stuck my hands down into my pockets and pulled out the rosary that Coraline had given me on the day of my Solemn Communion. I'd brought it along to recite "Our Father" and "Holy Mary, Mother of God, pray for us sinners" during Lila's funeral service. I lifted my head to look for signs in the sky. Heart-shaped clouds, living shapes bringing good tidings. But instead Lila's death loomed before me, like the walls—grown shabby over the years with graffiti and shreds of posters—that had replaced the sober gray walls of Danton Street, where we lived.

Lila passed away six months after our return from America. That morning she'd awakened feeling very fresh, yearning to eat one of the vegetable dishes that Henry prepared in the secret of his restaurant, The Kreyol, in downtown Manhattan. Lila had come back filled with firm resolutions, the need for an inner cleansing, and above all a sudden passion for vegetarian cooking. I think she wanted something with broccoli, brown rice, green peppers, seaweed, and tofu. The doctor examined her daily, but she was convinced that healthy food would save her old heart. She could already see herself getting off the plane in New York to celebrate Christmas with Henry.

She'd promised . . . We'd bought our tickets for New York . . . But Lila had gone off in search of a different sky. She left us on December 15.

3

Aside from being a soldier, the only other thing that Henry was good at was cooking. He grew up beside his mother Jenny's pots and pans, amid the steam and smell of cakes and fried food in the MacDowell kitchen. They were one of the richest British families in Saint John and had lived for more than four generations on the immense estate of Hamilton's Gardens. Jenny, having entered into the service of Mrs. MacDowell Senior at a tender age, consecrated her entire life to the MacDowells—and particularly to their only son, George MacDowell, who proved to be a formidable businessman, as his father had been. He spent half the year in England, owned a thriving textile factory in Manchester, flourmills in Liverpool, and import-export offices scattered throughout the English colonies.

George was fond of black women.

He'd always been surrounded by them, feasted his eyes upon them as they came and went with no corsets, or stockings, or garters, with low-necked camisoles that occasionally let a nipple slip out, wide skirts that they hitched up high on each side while they were doing the housework. They bathed naked standing in wooden tubs behind their cabins. As a child, he'd often sought refuge in the skirts of Peggy Douglas, Hamilton's Gardens' Baptist cook, who always found words to console him, told him Negro legends and stories about wily animals. As a teenager, he'd played doctor with Suzan and Rose, Peggy's two daughters.

George and Suzan even exchanged rings carved out of bamboo and promised to run away to England and get married far from the cold stares of the old portraits covering the walls of the vast residence at Hamilton's Gardens.

And then Jenny had come, after Augusta, Meredith, and Vanity, and many other young black girls, progeny of the poor folk of Saint John that vied for the rare privileged positions in the service of rich white people, in those cool shady homes where everyone spoke in hushed tones, walked at a measured pace, and counted neither the pounds nor the pence spent on a luncheon. In parlors where the tea, served at a fixed time in the afternoon, was poured by servants with civilized gestures, whose faces were not to divulge the slightest emotion. Aprons of fine lace. Immaculate white gloves offering with dignity moist muffins bulging with bits of candied fruit and currants on plates of English porcelain. Impassive Negresses, as invisible as possible, who were nothing but those white gloves and aprons. Heard nothing of the conversations of those charming and so terribly civilized ladies exchanging little sweet-salty words, organizing annual balls or lotteries, discussing works of charity and then whispering secrets leaning over their teacups. The ambiance was hushed, the laughter controlled, and the gestures restrained. You'd almost have thought you were in England if it weren't for the fleeting thoughts, like ugly blue flies, that landed every now and again with their dirty legs on the little cakes, causing visions to flit around the lovely rooms with varnished hardwood floors, visions of all those blue niggers milling around outside. Bad niggers sweating in the cane fields, fornicating or beating on one another, mouths filled with curse words, stinking of 110-proof rum.

While her daughters were away at school learning to become the first black Baptist schoolteachers in Saint John, Peggy Douglas was teaching Jenny the art of cooking. Peggy, hired into the kitchen of Hamilton's Gardens at the age of thirteen, was famous for her skill and her innate talent for teaching. And Mrs. MacDowell was proud to see her kitchens acquire the status of a school. A highly reputed place where, in the wink of an eye,

Peggy turned young, uneducated Negresses into choice cooks, "high-class" servants who might later, having acquired some experience and solid references, find a job anywhere in the English-speaking Caribbean where Mrs. MacDowell had relations.

"It is a veritable miracle every time; it's as if Peggy made a precious stone appear from a handful of dirt!" Mrs. MacDowell always exclaimed with renewed wonder.

In 1919, when Jenny walked through the terrifying gates of Hamilton's Gardens for the first time, George MacDowell was preparing to celebrate his sixteenth birthday. Jenny was fourteen. And she was definitely from the coarse earth that Mrs. MacDowell was so fond of evoking. The day she arrived, overwhelmed by the spaciousness, she wasn't able to utter a word, just stare in wonder and screw up her face with fright, hunch her shoulders up higher around her ears, crack her knuckles, and stumble over her own feet. When she set foot on the immense terrace paved with flagstones, her heart was beating so hard that she fainted.

One hour later, coming back from Bridgetown, George found her lying lifeless, head bleeding, in the same place. Her body was smooth and black, streaked with copper and bronze highlights that he so loved running his eyes or his fingertips over, such very white fingers on that black skin. He could have scooped her up, called for help, or even shaken her. But he felt only the desire to put his lips to Jenny's. Half-opened purple lips. The need to mold his body to her inanimate form and go to sleep lying atop her, sink into the same deep sleep. The urge to unbutton the blouse enclosing two firm breasts that yearned to see the light of day. To lift her skirts and smell the odor of the little wild creature hiding in her panties.

When Jenny opened her eyes, the first thing she saw was Michael's face, he was one of the grooms at Hamilton's Gardens. George MacDowell was standing three steps away, as if dumbstruck, arms dangling at his sides. He dared not make a move when Michael picked Jenny up, carried her to the outbuildings where the servants gave her herb tea and pressed cataplasms of leaves to her head.

In the following days Jenny did her best to grow accustomed to the luxury and magnificence of Hamilton's Gardens, to its long verandas, its Palladian windows, its Carrara marble, its paneled ceilings, its waxed hardwood floors . . . And to its silver teaspoons, its china, its lace, its velvet as well . . . Things sparkled in every corner, tinkled with clear splendor. A spotless, seamless world, where neither torn clothing nor mended linens existed. A closed world where life was never lived in haste nor the fear of want. But Jenny didn't have time for contemplating all of that. She just glanced at it furtively as she left the kitchen walking behind Peggy Douglas, scrutinizing her every move in order to learn as quickly as possible. Listen attentively to the soft-spoken advice of the elder woman, who separated each word distinctly to make herself understood and not have to repeat anything. Malleable and docile, Jenny was a talented student. Later she became Peggy's favorite and was often compared to Vanity, whom everyone considered to be Peggy's masterpiece. At that time—and for many years afterward—Vanity worked in Jamaica, on the Good Hope Plantation, at the residence of the incomparable Mr. and Mrs. Sharp.

"You going to do even better than Vany, I sure of it. You got what it takes," affirmed Peggy, who was usually sparing with her compliments. "And come three or four years, when you done with your apprenticeship, you might well find a job as head cook for a governor or a vice-consul, and get a chance at some good wages. You going to have to wait a bit longer for His Majesty King George V of Great Britain though!" she concluded soberly, tightening the knot of her apron over her broad, high-set buttocks.

Not long after that, Jenny was put in charge of preparing the small cakes that livened up the afternoon tea. In the evenings she was allowed to leaf carefully through Peggy's recipe books by candlelight: thirty years of calculated simmering, of sweet-sour delicacies and innovations, just to please the MacDowells.

From his early childhood, George was in the habit of passing through the kitchen to nibble on sweets or ask Peggy for a glass of lemonade. But ever since Jenny's arrival, he was there every day, used any pretense to see her, gaze hungrily at her body, sound out her eyes. At the time, the mere sight of a MacDowell made Jenny tremble. And that particular MacDowell was worse than the others . . . He aroused strange feelings within her. She hoped he would come and yet did her best to avoid running into him. She yearned to feel him next to her, but kept him at a distance all the while. She sought to catch his eye without acknowledging his smile. And to touch him, God! Just to touch him . . . So she awaited him, furious at herself and at him when he'd suddenly appear—always ravenous, dying of thirst.

It didn't take Peggy long to notice the strange antics that were humming their little tune around her stove. One day, she lectured Jenny: "I don't know what that MacDowell boy's up to, but if I got one piece of advice to give you, it's don't even set eyes on him. He a decent boy and he got nothing against us black folk. When he was a child, I used to tell him our folktales. He ran around like a pup between my legs with my two daughters, Suzan and Rose, they almost saved today, on the verge of becoming schoolteachers. Watch out for yourself, Jenny! One don't need to fear the bite of them kind of animals when they young! But now he getting to the age when his teeth growing long. Long teeth that can bite you, Jenny! You know white folk just grow them teeth naturally with time . . . And also, poor child, the thing he got in his pants, it's a toy all right, but it ain't made of wood! And it seems to me it's got the sort of hankerings you might guess. So stay away from him, you hear? Blouse buttoned up, legs closed tight! . . . And don't go around without no panties on neither!"

From that day onward, Jenny bowed her head and kept her eyes on the floor as soon as George stuck his nose in the kitchen. She could clearly imagine the long fangs hiding behind his thin pink lips, and most of all, she saw the toy inside his pants rising, swelling, and lifting its head. To rid herself of those visions, all Jenny had to do was close her eyes very tightly and send all those fiendish sights back to their dark den.

It was an act of providence, in association with Peggy's prayers, that James Henry MacDowell decided to send his son to England for a year. In his opinion, George needed to put everything he'd learned into practice. They had in fact spent hours and hours in the secrecy of his vast office where the files of work-in-progress were piled in stacks: a phenomenal amount of paperwork, crawling with numbers that he alone could decipher.

George was eighteen years old. The day before his departure, he came prowling around the kitchen one last time, "like a dog marking his territory," Peggy recalled several years later. She often told that story, bursting with helpless rage, far from the ears of Hamilton's Gardens, forgetting for a moment that she was Mrs. MacDowell's respectable cook, forgetting that she was one of the most dignified representatives of the Baptist Church, the pious and fervent Peggy Douglas, forgetting that her daughters Suzan and Rose were the only two black schoolteachers in all of Saint John.

After having inspected the kitchen by running his fingers over the buffets, George found nothing to nibble on. So he ran up to Peggy Douglas, put his arms around her shoulders, like he might have done in the old days. Peggy struggled weakly against him, just the right amount—for she knew how to keep her place—forced a laugh, even if on that particular day her heart was not joyous. Surprised, Jenny lifted her head. And that's how her eyes met those of George.

"Are you going to let me go, Master George?" Peggy implored in a childish voice, stamping her feet on the red clay tiles. "I got work to do, Master George!" Despite her tall stature and natural authority, Peggy often affected that childlike tone of voice in the presence of a MacDowell.

But George wasn't listening to her anymore. Jenny's eyes were filling with water. And he dove in and swam in that water. He imagined he was the captain of a ship sailing on that sea. Imagined that he was an explorer of new worlds, lost in that immensity. He would have liked to take Jenny by the hand, lead her away from Hamilton's Gardens, where everything was so demanding, filled with starchy conventions, British to the point of being ridiculous. A prisoner, that was all he was! Hands and feet tied to his rank, to the privileges that his white skin conferred upon him . . . But he was still a MacDowell, so he pulled himself together and ran out of the pantry calling: "Wait for me, little Jenny! Promise you'll wait for me! I'll be back . . ."

"All them folk know how to do is give orders!" Peggy said to herself, filled with bitterness and spite. "They not only wanting the sweat off your brow, but your brow itself so they can mark it and show that you is their property, and even your brow ain't enough: they got to have your head too so that they can stuff it with their own ideas. And then you can grant them your arms and legs too, and what's between your thighs! And that ain't enough, offer them your heart and cherish them more than your own parents who suffered to bring you out of misery . . . Get along! Good riddance, Master George! Bon voyage, and may God save you and the king to boot!" she concluded in a hushed voice.

That's how George's words stuck in Jenny's mind. And nothing ever succeeded in prying them loose. She waited for him for a whole year, slowly maturing in Mrs. MacDowell's kitchen. With a glad heart, filled with dreams, she laughed and sang from morning till night. Each meal made for the MacDowells bore the mark of her joyfulness. The dishes she prepared sang out her name: Jenny! The roasted meats that had rather been Peggy's specialty before, also celebrated her name: Jenny!

"Jenny! You are one of nature's wonders!" exclaimed Mrs. MacDowell biting into the small cakes flavored with vanilla or ginger. "God is great indeed! And I believe we needn't despair for your race!"

Jenny had changed. Her curves had filled out in her sixteenth year. She seemed taller, but in fact she simply stood straighter, walked with her head up and held her breasts high. The black men in Hamilton's Gardens, all crowded around her now. And Michael, Mr. MacDowell's favorite groom, the one who'd come to her aid the day she first arrived, even asked for her hand in marriage.

Peggy appreciated Michael. A Baptist, as she was, the young

mulatto-*chabin* had been singing in the choir at the church with the same fervor since he was a small child. Even though Jenny never spoke of Master George, Peggy knew. She'd lived long enough on this earth to be able to detect a smitten heart, fleshly transports, or even small torments of the soul. She knew very well that Jenny didn't feel anything of the kind for Michael, but she pushed the one to pop the question and the other to accept. In her opinion, it was the surest way to save Jenny from the spell that George MacDowell had cast upon her, spare her future disappointment and disillusions.

In the bit of life she'd spent at Hamilton's Gardens, Jenny had never refused anything to Peggy Douglas. She couldn't hold up under the woman's lecturing and promised to marry Michael before the end of December. A baptized Catholic, she immediately began Bible studies in order to convert to the Baptist religion, enter into the true faith, and rid her soul of young MacDowell's words, the words of a white man, she mustn't forget that!

"What he going to do for you, Jenny? Nothing at all. God is my witness, I did everything in my power to get them dreams out of your head! White folk with white folk. Black folk with black folk, Jenny! And the world will keep on turning round . . ."

Michael wasn't a black man, but a very light-skinned *chabin,* with wooly hair the color of dried straw. Peggy placed him in the category of black men because he belonged to the group that served the others, bowed down, and knew nothing but obedience. The group of people who had risen from the infamous cabins, the cane fields, the dark ship holds, who sang hallelujah with her in the choir at the Baptist church and lived in the hope of a new sun in a different sky. Michael's mother, a Negress from the Holton District, worked as a chambermaid at Greenfield Park, in the austere household of a very refined gentleman, Brandon Robinson. A well-known homosexual, he now resided more often in his manor house in Shrewsbury, England than on the island of Saint John where, according to his doctor, the hot and humid climate hardly agreed with him. No one knew who

Michael's father was, but people whispered that it was Master Brandon's own brother, an inveterate gambler who had once retired to Greenfield Park to dodge his London creditors.

Encouraged by Peggy, the young couple hurried to get engaged three days before George returned. It was done very simply—just a plum pudding and a quick kiss on the cheek—for Jenny and Peggy were already busy in the outbuildings feverishly preparing for the sumptuous dinner party that Mrs. MacDowell was holding for her closest friends in honor of George's homecoming. Sixty guests! More than twenty courses! Young black girls requisitioned from all over the estate to accomplish domestic chores, while Peggy and Jenny excelled in their art.

George had grown taller, his shoulders were broader and his voice deeper, but living in England had lent a greenish tinge to his complexion. He'd become the very portrait of his maternal grandfather, Jonathan Whitworth, who had been presiding over the parlor in his finely gilt frame for nearly fifty years. George had come home to Hamilton's Gardens, and everything was dazzling, astonishing, and new. He could no longer imagine living anywhere else on earth, only here with his black men and women. Especially his black women, the ones who'd washed and pampered, fed and spoiled him, served him and tucked him in, day after day, throughout the wonderful years of his childhood. His only wish was to be surrounded once again by their solicitude, their gracefulness, their black hands on his white skin, their smiles, always only half finished, their submissive words.

He appeared around six o'clock, right when the kitchen was in a state of great agitation: delicious steamy smells, anguished cries, talk of curdled sauces, imminent calamities lying in ambush at the bottom of saucepans, jellies to watch, the coming and going of steaming kettles, and the fear of burning a roast fowl . . . First he went and gave Peggy a kiss; she mimicked welcoming gestures as she pushed him away. There were so many black women gathered there that he thought he was in one of the dreams he used to have in London. Each woman was wearing a white handkerchief on her head. Their skin shone with sweat. There were so many breasts bobbing around. So many buttocks filling out skirts authoritatively. So many black arms, legs, and thighs mingled. A forest of bodies!

He recognized Jenny from her eyes.

The same as the ones that had moved him the year before, filled with water. They said: "I waited for you, Master George MacDowell. I'm yours for eternity . . ."

The dinner was a triumph and lasted nearly six hours. It was torture for George who imagined himself growing blacker in the eyes of the guests the more he thought about his Jenny's body. As if his guilty thoughts were oozing from his pores, spreading and growing in dark splotches on his skin. But no one noticed his discomfort. Conversations were lively amidst the clinking silverware. And he put on a brilliant act himself. He made his parents proud by relating in very witty terms the comical adventures he'd been through with those incredible Englishmen from England who had not exactly proven to be models of good upbringing. Yet he had become a man over there, in the London smog. And his mother Elizabeth MacDowell was seriously thinking of choosing a wife for him amongst the wealthiest young women on the island, who could be counted on the fingers of one hand.

Later, at the hour when night spirits deserted the gardens of the Hamilton Estate, George opened his eyes, jumped out of bed, and went to scratch like a dog at Jenny's door. Luck was with him. Gloria, who usually shared the cabin, had gone to meet a man named Eliott Pigmare, a servant from the Blue South Estate who only deigned to rub shoulders with the servants and chambermaids from the richest residences in Saint John. At least fifteen children now called him "Daddy Pig." And it's true, he did look a little like a pig with his pointed ears, his tragic smile, and his plump belly. But no one really understood how, without using witchcraft or trickery, he inspired love in women's hearts.

Jenny had just gotten home a few minutes earlier. They'd had to clean up the kitchen, the china, and the crystal. First she sat down on the edge of her cot, then flopped back completely dressed, arms heavy, neck stiff, and her head still buzzing from those three frantic days of preparation. Her feet were swollen, and she didn't have the strength to lift them onto the bed. Sleep, that's what she needed, she thought to herself. When George suddenly appeared in her thoughts, she jumped, and, to keep herself from sinning, began to repeat immediately: "Engaged! I'm already engaged! Oh Lord! Bring this lost sheep back to your fold!"

As the figure of George began to fill her mind, she spread her legs and tried to call Michael to her aid. Michael, the husband that Peggy Douglas had found for her. But Michael did not appear, not even in George's shadow, George whose presence was now all-encompassing.

"Engaged! Engaged! I'm engaged to Michael!"

Flopped down there like a rag doll, it seemed as if she'd passed away. But a tempest was raging within her and breaking down the complex scaffolding that Peggy had so patiently built up with great perseverance, endlessly repeated words, and faith in God . . . "White folk with white folk, and black folk with black folk, and the world will keep on turning round. You hear me, Jenny! He won't do nothing for you!"

Jenny tried to think of George's faults so she could feel disgusted with him, push his face away. She insulted him, digging up dirty words she hadn't used since she'd been living at Hamilton's Gardens. In her imagination, she hit him, made fun of his greenish complexion. But instead it was as if she were summoning him. Suddenly he was at her door, whispering her name, begging her to open her heart to him.

If Mrs. Elizabeth MacDowell had seen her son—her daily source of wonder—scratching at Jenny's door that night, she would have undoubtedly choked, forgotten to breathe, and her life would have been snuffed out on the spot. Thank God she was sleeping peacefully in her apartments, on her three cotton mattresses, in her vast mahogany bed with cabled bedposts, under the fixed and protective gaze of her old dead aunts who had posed for the same portrait painter twenty-five years earlier. Her breathing was regular and the pale faces of young women filing past her filled her dreams. Smiles of immaculate virgins under flowered parasols trimmed with lace.

When George pushed open the door, Jenny wasn't startled. It was all in the order of things. There had always been an invisible bond between the two of them. They exchanged but few words. They needed to be inside one another more than anything else. As deep down inside as possible. They wanted to mingle their saliva, their arms, their legs, their blood. Touch one another. Kiss one another over and over. He sucked on her breasts, sucked until the milk of love began to rise. Then he held in his mouth the little wild creature with black hair that she kept tucked between her legs. And Jenny, who had no practice in the motions of lovemaking, performed them naturally with him, invented them for him. She let herself go, basked in pleasure. Arched her back and undulated with George MacDowell. There was no more cot, no more mud floor, no more candle stuck on the ground. Nothing but Jenny and George. Violent hungry kisses. Sweat. Cries. Enflamed words that heralded infinite, eternal love paraded about in broad daylight. Caresses that promised their two bodies could never be separated, like the two symmetrical sides of those unfolded cutout paper hearts that hung in garlands in Peggy's Baptist church.

When Gloria found them in the morning, sleeping knotted up together, she held back a scream. Three days earlier, under Peggy Douglas's authoritative eye, she had partaken of the modest plum pudding that marked Jenny and Michael's engagement.

Gloria pulled on one of Jenny's toes. But George awoke first. He sat up like a shipwrecked sailor on his raft drifting in the middle of the ocean. Poor lost soul who suddenly sights, jutting up on the barren horizon, unknown continents and islands. He looked dumbfounded, happy, and dazed. In his stupefaction, all he could manage to mumble was: "Oh!" as if he'd just arrived at his destination. "Oh!" surprised that his journey was over. He hurriedly slipped on his clothing. Then he fled.

Outside batches of Negroes and Negresses were busying themselves around the outbuildings. Everyone saw him. Come out of Jenny's cabin. Stride quickly away. Jump over the tubs of soapy water where the embroidered tablecloths from the dinner party were soaking. Escape the gnashing teeth of dogs quarreling over the lamb bones. Nearly slip in the grass, moist with morning dew. Strike out at a run with his open shirt flapping behind him, his pants on backward, and his blond hair flopping down on his forehead. He ran past Michael's stony gaze as well, the unfortunate man could already hear Jenny's name passing from mouth to mouth in the pained laughter of the Negroes from Hamilton's Gardens.

Two hours later, George was sitting in front of his breakfast, sipping little gulps of Darjeeling. Showered, decked out in a suit and tie, his fingers were gathering up little piles of crumbs on the tablecloth as he listened distractedly to his mother to whom the night had revealed a certain Kathleen Wolsey.

"An excellent choice, George! Think about it . . ."

"Mother, I'm not thinking about getting married. This Miss Wolsey is undoubtedly an exquisite young woman. But, if you don't mind, I need a few more years to get the hang of the business world."

"The two are not necessarily incompatible, George!"

"Mother!" And he laughed loudly as he put down his cup. "I've never even met this dear young woman, Kathleen. What makes you think she'd want to have anything to do with me?"

"Silly boy! You know perfectly well we're speaking of a rich heiress, George, and an only child as well . . . She'd be perfect . . ."

"Mother, forgive me! But I've just come back from England . . . You're not even allowing me the time to get accustomed to Hamilton's Gardens again."

With those words he fell silent. Through the Palladian windows, the sun danced in the leaves of the ancient trees. George smiled as he thought of the dogs that almost sunk their teeth into his calves as he was running back to the house.

"Promise me you'll think about it, George! It will please me so much. I'll speak to your father at dinner and . . ."

"Please, Mother. It's out of the question!" he interrupted as the memory of one of those Negroes in the old days who'd been torn to pieces by the dogs suddenly flashed through his mind.

A panting black man, with one hand cut off, his face covered with old scars poorly stitched together and newer, bloody wounds. When the dogs had let go of him, the lashing of whips made him dance in front of a circle of white men who snickered as the Negro screamed, danced, wheeled around, jumped, begging pity from mankind, from God, and from death too.

That event had taken place in an era George had never known. But in his nightmares, he often saw such horrid scenes, as if they still haunted the estate, impregnated it, tainted it, like permanent indelible stains on Hamilton's Gardens. Sometimes, it was enough to simply prick up your ears to bring back the screams of the old days, superpose the wounds of centuries of slavery on the tales he remembered from childhood. Then infernal clamors rose to fill the friendly silences of the estate with horror. They came rushing up, like furious hordes. And the crowds chained up there, eyes like hunted beasts, were a terrible sight. A terrible sight, those Negroes hanging from the branches of those handsome, imperturbable trees, feigning amnesia, while their leaves fluttered in the warm breeze, endlessly whispering the names of Percy, Garry, and so many others.

"Poor Michael! That's all anyone's talking about, Jenny! The shame you put on him! Poor fellar! Didn't deserve this, Michael didn't . . . Soon as I had my back turned, you done erased the engagement from your mind . . ."

Head bowed, hands wringing behind her back, Jenny stood very straight in front of Peggy.

"You don't know that slavery was abolished in 1800 and something? You don't know that you is someone who can say no? You don't know that, eh? You got the right to refuse . . . No, Master George! I engaged to a nice boy named Michael Landworth, and he's a right decent man. And you mustn't go shaming him, because it will break his heart. His name is Michael, Master George, and I got a right to cut off what's itching you with a knife, Master George . . . I got a right to break that little toy of yours . . . eh, Jenny? You didn't find nothing to say. You just lay down and gave him everything he came looking for . . . Oh God! I can always feel them things coming; it's incredible and don't take much smoke . . . What got into you, Jenny? Black folk with black folk, white folk with white folk, and the world will keep on turning round . . ."

"Black folk with black folk, white folk with white folk," Jenny repeated after her, almost mechanically, like the verses of the Bible whose mysteries she didn't understand even though—she was firmly convinced—they held an essential truth about life on earth and promised eternity in some other heaven.

"Yes absolutely: black folk with black folk! And don't let no white man sail up to you!" Peggy scolded and struck the flour barrel with her wooden spoon.

"Black folk with black folk, white folk with white folk, Miss Peggy! And don't let no white man come sailing up to you . . . Black folk with . . ."

Jenny knew she'd behaved wrongly toward Michael. Simply thinking about it made a knot form deep down in her stomach . . . Poor Michael! Just the fact of associating Michael with the word "poor" upset her. Poor Michael, it was a chain that Peggy, and even she, systematically hung on his name . . . Poor Michael, whose immense misfortune was set in every crease in Peggy's face, in her mouth twisted with disappointment, in her eyes that reflected hate and despair. Poor Michael!

Terribly dismayed but not feeling the slightest regret, Jenny started stirring the batter for the little five o'clock fruitcakes more energetically, repeating to herself that Peggy was right: "Black folk with black folk, white folk with white folk!" Unfortunately, other unbridled thoughts hopped over that reasoning, which had been wrought in the history of Saint John and loomed as high as the iron bars of the imposing gate to Hamilton's Gardens. And Jenny said to herself that the world had kept on turning round while she and George MacDowell had given themselves to one another. A new day had dawned. With the same sun. She'd found Miss Peggy busy with the same pots and pans . . . She could still feel George's hands on her skin, his breath and his kisses. She regretted nothing about her night. With very few words, they had promised each other everything. Deep down inside, in the dark depths where Peggy Douglas's bitterness never went, Jenny was calm and serene. Her mouth chewed the words of repentance as she'd been ordered to, but her heart beat for George MacDowell.

"I going to talk with Michael," Peggy declared wiping her forehead. "I going to lie for you, Jenny. Afterwards, you say the same thing, eh? That Master George had been drinking."

"Yes, that he'd been drinking."

"That he didn't know where he was."

"Yes, that he didn't know where he was, Miss Peggy."

"That he fell on the floor at the foot of your bed."

"Yes, that he fell on the floor at the foot of my bed . . ."

"And that nothing happened between you. Nothing at all!!! Nothing at all!!!"

"Nothing at all!" mumbled Jenny hesitantly. "Nothing at all! Nothing happened between us, Miss Peggy.

"And you'll swear to it on the Bible! And you'll marry Michael and not lose no time in making him happy. And if the other left a seed, since Michael is a *chabin,* no one will know the difference . . ." Peggy assured, brandishing her wooden spoon like a cross.

Alas, Jenny did not need to recite a single one of those lies. Michael spared her the trouble. The next morning, three Negroes unstrung his body from the thickest branch of one of the four ancient trees planted in front of the veranda at Hamilton's Gardens.

No one had seen him all day. Furious, not knowing what had happened, Mr. MacDowell had sent people out to look for him all over the estate. Michael had run off on Columbus, his magnificent stallion that no one—not even George—was allowed to ride. Michael had galloped far from Hamilton's Gardens, constantly urging the horse on with renewed rage. They say he made sparks fly from the horse's hooves. People saw him in three different places at the same time. In front of Greenfield Park where his mother worked. There, he rang the bell and disappeared immediately, his face bathed in tears and sweat mingled together. At Bayside, his yellow hair sticking up on his head, he asked a young boy from south of River Rocks for a swallow of water. And then, facing out to sea, appealing to the setting sun, he hurled out his pain. Some saw his soul break loose and fly away, while his inanimate body remained sitting on Columbus's back. Others said that he'd been dead since morning when he heard Jenny's name stuck to Master George's going from mouth to mouth. His soul had left him at that very moment. Though Michael galloped after it all day, he hadn't been able to catch up with it. And those who were best informed claimed that Jenny had best start worrying right away, for Michael's tormented soul would never grow weary of prowling around her.

Michael didn't return to Hamilton's Gardens until nightfall. He galloped around the huge house three times before throwing the rope over a branch. He must have had to do some incredible gymnastics in order to hang himself. Climb up in the tree. Tie the rope around his neck. Stand up on Columbus's back. And then jump. Let himself swing. His feet pedaling in the air for a moment.

The next morning, before taking him down, there were lengthy comments about the manner in which Michael had put an end to his life. People cast worried looks at Columbus, the sole witness to Michael's last journey. Clear-eyed, the horse stood grazing on green moss several feet away. All they found in Michael's pockets was a dead bird. Very stiff, like Michael, but its feet were curled up and its wings ruffled. A little bird that you could hold in a closed hand. Upon seeing it, everyone thought of the slaves, Percy and Nanny, who were legendary in the Negro cabins on the estate.

The two lovers from another era had chosen death over being separated. But it was said their love had been so strong that it didn't die with them. It continued to live on in the body of a bird.

For three days, until the day of the funeral, Peggy didn't say a word to Jenny. She kept her grief pent up inside. Grief nursed with selected, painful thoughts she kept rehashing in her mind. The memory of Michael as a child exulting in the church choir. His little white socks hiked right up to his knees. Poor Michael! The way he used to have of opening his eyes so wide when he was singing hymns, making the congregation lay down the load of their misery and walk in the light of hope. Poor Michael! The plum pudding of his engagement to Jenny. His long fingers with bluish nails. Poor Michael, he never opened up his heart, but he made sure his life was drawn in a straight line that led directly to the house of God. He imagined himself with a beautiful family in the future. Poor Michael, he even pictured himself as an old man, with his lovely Jenny, surrounded by grandchildren . . . Peggy went over these memories endlessly, stifling the suffering within her. Didn't share it. That pain was hers. It helped her and strengthened her faith in the idea that her race was cursed.

"The man we buried three months ago is the father of the child you carrying," she announced to Jenny when she realized the girl was pregnant. You tell that to everyone and even to the man who visits you every night.

"I can't say that, Miss Peggy," protested Jenny.

"Why can't you?" exclaimed Peggy with a start, not in the habit of being contradicted.

"You know why, Miss Peggy . . ."

"You think he going to marry you?"

"I didn't say that . . ."

"Then why?" cried Peggy flopping down on a bench.

She stared at Jenny more sternly than she had since Michael's death. "You nuts, poor girl." An annoyed smile flashed across her lips. "You think George MacDowell loves you? You think a MacDowell can divorce himself from his rank for a little Negress? You just one of his vices. You know, some folk always go back to the buffet where the whiskey bottle is hid. They just can't help it. Well, you best get that into your head, Jenny. He comes to you just like he'd go to the buffet where old James Henry MacDowell hides his whiskey—out of vice. He takes you. He drinks your body right down to the last drop. Until he can't walk straight and sees all the animals in the Great Ark, until he vomits up his guts. You nothing but George MacDowell's vice, Jenny. Does anyone marry a bottle, Jenny? No, they keep it closed up in the dark cupboard. And take it out when no one is looking, Jenny. They know it's a vice, so they shamed, Jenny! And poor Michael is dead because of that . . . You ain't heard nothing about a marriage between white folk lately? You should keep your ears open, child! Well one of these nights when he comes to suck on his vice, ask him who he getting married to. And remind him that vice begets posterity too. And that he'll soon have a MacDowell heir to introduce to his mother."

That night George broke down on Jenny's shoulder. He wept over the life he'd poured into his Negress's body, just when love became so violent that the veins in his temples suddenly stood out, looking like strange little painful green lizards. His jaws grew stiff. He incarnated another George MacDowell, liberated from his parents, the descendants of slave-driving plantation owners who—immortal and austere on the walls—stared at everyone, watched, judged, inspired Hamilton's Gardens. That other George, ecstatic, penetrated Jenny's body like he would go into a forbidden forest. And all the love that he felt for her assuaged his tormented visions, dangled the shimmering hope of a healing path before him. Though they'd never spoken of Michael's death, George and Jenny each thought about it in private, always with a feeling of uneasiness that stemmed from remorse.

Does anyone marry a bottle, Jenny?

Because he was the true heir of his father James Henry MacDowell and of his mother the very honorable Elizabeth MacDowell, a fervent Catholic, whose genealogical tree, on her grandmother's side, mingled its leaves and branches with that of Queen Victoria, he allowed his family to ask, on his behalf, for the hand of Kathleen, whom he married in 1923.

No! They keep the whiskey closed up in a dark cupboard . . .

Very white, delicate, and infinitely diaphanous, Kathleen was the daughter of the venerable Edward Wolsey III, a widower, art lover, specialist in Shakespeare, independently wealthy penny pincher, and the owner of a sumptuous stud farm in Scotland that bred exceptional horses, which the wealthy families of Europe fought to acquire. His grandfather had invested a fortune in the construction of the Suez Canal, just when Lesseps was running into his worst difficulties. Because of that, Kathleen was passionately interested in Egypt.

The whiskey bottle is nothing but a vice! People are shamed of it, Jenny!

Henry was born in the month of December of that same year. He grew up at Hamilton's Gardens, enveloped in the respect everyone felt for poor dead Michael—his supposed father—and in his mother Jenny's love, who devoted her life to culinary art. In New York, behind his pots and pans, Henry became a master just like Jenny. And with time, he realized that he had probably tried all his life to recreate the atmosphere and the smells of the kitchen at Hamilton's Gardens. After having left Lila in Paris in 1946, he'd opened his first Creole restaurant in Houston and married Lana, a mulattress from Trinidad. Lana dreamt of going to New York. So they went north in 1952. The Kreyol Food, which was founded on Third Street, quickly built up a reliable clientele of West Indians and black Americans. In 1970, Lana died of lung cancer, leaving him alone with four children. Three boys, one girl.

And then in 1972, Henry moved his restaurant again. Coming home from the market one Indian summer day, he'd gone down a street he didn't usually take. Passersby, crowding in front of what looked like an antique shop, were buying little useless, worn, or cracked objects, perfume bottles, makeup cases, cups, and teaspoons. The shop itself was for sale too. Guided by bright beams of sunlight, Henry walked through the shop and found an interior courtyard where city birds dwelled.

"Love at first sight!" he explained to those who were nostalgic for The Kreyol Food on Third Street.

He declared himself a vegetarian after he'd been told all the damaging effects of meat. Man had walked on the moon for the first time. It was the eve of the enormous civil rights demonstrations. The hippy movement was in full swing. Martin Luther

King was already a myth. The war in Vietnam was on the front page of the *New York Times*. After that The Kreyol Food was simply called The Kreyol.

4

Long ago, in Guadeloupe, I had another mother.

Black.

As black as Lila was white.

When both of them were on my mind, they were always bumping up against one another. Two enemy marbles that you wished would shatter into a thousand pieces. Black against white. White against black. Over and over again.

That mother also had hard-boned hands. Harder than Lila's. Yellowed nails cut short. The whites of her black eyes were very white, frightening. Long pointed purple lips like a beak. She was tall, dried-up, neck craned. She walked just like those women who possess nothing, have lost all hope of latching onto a chance in life. At the same pace, she would walk up to meet everything that was set in front of her—good or bad—unsmiling, dry-eyed, two creases furrowed smack in the middle of her brow.

Seemingly hardened to life, Noémie knew how to put up a front. People thought of her as being strong, but she was fragile. Cracked and dented inside. Even before she lost her husband and the child she was bearing.

She would stand there in life with her arms dangling. Proud and dignified, without really knowing why anymore. A pride that held her up straight, as if in a corset. She ate earth, heard voices, shooed away invisible forms that flitted past her face. She spoke of Robert and her dead baby boy. Thought they were alive, waited for them to come back. She seemed to have neither ties nor trammels and that lent elegance to each of her gestures, a sort of regal blitheness.

That was the way she left me one day with Coraline and Judes in Point-à-Pitre. We all sat down in the shade of the veranda in the wicker chairs. Anne-Lise, the maid, served ice-cold orangeade. I remember how the words slipped by over my head. And while those delicate and charming people who were to become my parents caressed my cheeks and hair, Noémie whispered: "Nine years ago, Robert and I named her Sybille. But it doesn't matter if you feel like changing her name. Do whatever you like. She's yours now. Robert didn't have any objection to it. He has his little boy to warm his heart . . ."

That's all I can remember of what she said. After that, she hadn't shared any more words. She looked at the sky, gazed strangely at the sun. Stood up. Gave me a kiss on the forehead. Her lips were dry and pointed, her fingers rough. Her eyes looked through me one last time. And then she walked away, borne along on the wind, airy and majestic with her flowered dress swirling around her long black legs. Pushed far away from me with her two arms swinging on each side of her body, like wings. She'd rid herself of me, didn't even turn around.

"Sybille, I named her Sybille . . . She's yours . . . Robert didn't have any objection to it . . ."

I never forgot her pointed dry lips, her rough hands, her raving sentences, her eyes that no longer saw me.

I was nine years old. It was in 1963, two years after they'd found the two bodies in that room, not far from the harbor in Basse-Terre. My father Robert and the girl Clothilde, naked, wrapped around one another, dead.

Every time someone came to visit, Judes and Coraline would mention it, in muffled tones, glance furtively at me with pity in their eyes. Their visitors immediately cast the same wet smiles at me, murmuring soft and compassionate words that I could clearly hear, as if they came floating over separately one at a time, velvet petals, goose down, and settled right up against my ears . . .

"Oh! My God! Oh! Dear Lord!" moaned Coraline. "Poor Child. Her papa's dead. Her little brother was stillborn. And her mama will die in the asylum. She's been locked up over there a long time, thinking her dead have been resuscitated and are alive . . ."

"Poor Sybille! Her papa went searching for life. And it was death he found: the price of sin . . .

"Poor *ti moun,* she's got no one left, no father, no mother, no brother," the friends repeated in chorus.

"God is merciful, she met you on her path . . ."

Two young bodies intertwined on a bed. Naked. Only a narrow white satin ribbon tied around the girl's neck, a small gold chain on one ankle, and one of those delicate Creole rosebuds placed in her mouth. She had her eyes open, her gaze suspended in ecstasy. She hadn't had time to be afraid, undoubtedly hadn't seen the end coming. She hadn't suffered, and you could tell she'd gone in the height of love-making, her abdomen offered up, her breasts well-kneaded and her legs spread wide to receive the man, let him come inside of her. His body was covering hers completely. Magnificently outlined and shiny, the muscles of his back had remained tensed with the effort of that ultimate embrace. It didn't really seem as if they'd been interrupted but rather stopped short. Their bodies had no cutlass, rifle, punch, or kick marks on them. They were united—a frozen image—in love and the enigma of their beautifully peaceful death.

The girl's name was Clothilde. Was barely twenty years old . . . When she was seven, she'd started telling dreams. Her mother, Gérémise, immediately remembered that Néhémie, her grandmother's sister, had the gift of interpreting dreams. After that discovery, everyone held Clothilde in great respect, guessing, supposing, suspecting at one and the same time that behind those childish features lay the wisdom and technique of the old woman who left this life on her ninety-fifth birthday . . .

The day before her death, Néhémie had walked out to the most distant savannahs in Saint-Jean to say goodbye to her family and friends. She begged them above all not to shed any tears, but simply to throw flowers into her coffin. "Lots of flowers, please!" she implored so that she would still smell sweet when she reached the other shore. Without the hint of a quaver in her voice, she dictated her last will and testament. Put her affairs in order. And paid for the notarized will.

To her nephews and niece, she was leaving two plots of land on the slopes of Grosse-Roche and her cabin filled with collections of dreams that were not visible to the eye, that didn't exist in the same way as flesh and blood beings did, but that one was always mysteriously bumping into. Mingled scents, flowery or sacrilegious, nauseating or sweet.

Twice during her career, dream characters had escaped their delimitations and appeared in the visible world. Transformed into a fury, Néhémie had run them out like a couple of tired old fiends, with a few good kicks and curses, proving to everyone that she did indeed have great mastery over dreams. When she died, no one wanted the cabin in question.

To those who were astonished at the utter calm with which she announced her imminent death, Néhémie answered that a person's time on earth had a beginning and an end. She'd lived her days fully and was leaving without the slightest regret. Hearing these chilling words, grown men suddenly turned back into boys and shuddered. When Néhémie left them, they ran to warm their insides with a good shot of fiery rum. Others, who were bolder, pressed her to name the sign or the dream that had enlightened her about the day of her death. Néhémie closed her eyes. Then she shook her head just like a child who has made a solemn promise.

"All I can tell you," she repeated in her wonderfully composed way, "is that this life's got a beginning and an end. My day is coming tomorrow, that's all . . . Don't worry, I lived a full life. I have no regrets . . ."

After having philosophically pronounced these evident facts, she retired in silence. Then everyone became scathingly aware of being utterly helpless in the face of destiny and terrified as well at the idea that time was not inexhaustible like the water in the rivers, eternal like the morning sun that always overcomes the darkness. Some people felt as if they were caught in a vice, devastated at having wasted time and still more time than all the gray hairs on their heads. A few, decaying and flaccid, made firm resolutions—promised themselves to economize their days, not lend a single crumb to anyone, wisely fill up the rest of their lives, and die in churchly serenity, following the example of Dame Néhémie.

After she'd made her rounds, the old woman cleaned up her cabin, washed herself, and put on the new purple taffeta dress that a young seamstress cousin had made for her years before. Then she calmly stretched out on her bed. Death would carry her away three hours after midday.

During her long life, Néhémie had not known a single man. Of course, she'd had opportunities. But she'd preferred to devote her life to doing good deeds. Never calculating or asking favors, never even demanding as much as a penny, she delivered unfortunate people from the Devil's clutches. She healed invisible wounds, turned away evil spirits. She couldn't even count the number of innocent beings she'd brought back to life. Every night, Néhémie dreamed profusely. Dreaming was her life, her truth, her joy, her paradise. It was like walking out in the bright noonday sun. According to her, interpreting dreams was as simple as pulling open a curtain to let the sunshine in, for her gaze came to rest upon the table of darkness like a lamp. A generous woman, she also dreamed for others who got lost on the paths of sleep and saw the morning steal away with the keys they'd been given during the night.

Néhémie could differentiate one dream from another; she classified them by categories depending upon their texture, their origin, and their destination . . . Omen-dreams sent by angels, evil-dreams dispatched by demons, premonition-dreams, useless-dreams in which the body takes possession of the spirit, trinket-dreams, veil-and-lace-dreams behind which dwell the real-authentic dreams, chasm-dreams heralding a fall, dreams of the dead and the living, dreams of jars full of gold, travel-and-white-ocean-liner-dreams, dreams of the Virgin Mary and Jesus Christ, dreams of pulled teeth, dreams in the red-white-and-blue of France-Paradise . . .

When Néhémie lay down to sleep her last sleep, she started counting—like one would count sheep—the number of thank-yous she'd received for her interpretations. Satisfied, waiting patiently with her hands joined on her stomach, she lay smiling in her bed. And then—the mind is a wanderer—suddenly, her whole life passed before her eyes. Her mother, the time she spent at the school in Saint-Jean . . . Lastly, the grimacing faces of two or three suitors who had attempted to get a peek under her white skirts.

"You going to regret it!" One of them, whose name was Clodomir, had predicted. "Later, when your hair's gray and your skin crumpled up, maybe you'll dream of me . . . but that'll be too late! For, you see, my dear, dreaming ain't enough, you got to live things to understand the world . . . Everybody round here kisses your virgin feet and your heart's fulfilled. You living with their praise like it's your only nourishment, your sole treasure, but believe my words, Néné! In truth, your heart is shut up tight and love's a foreign sweet to your soul . . . You'll be crying one day, Néné!"

Néhémie had never felt the slightest regret. Once, thirty years ago, she'd even dreamed that Marga, Clodomir's eldest daughter, was wandering around naked in the forest. Had been bitten by a rat. But instead of red human blood, clear river water ran from the wound, and upon it floated a white boat. Clodomir's daughter was sobbing and trying to hold back the flow. Alas, the force of the rushing waters kept pushing her hands away.

The very next day, Néhémie took it upon herself to transmit her interpretation to Marga, whom she found sitting alone at the foot of a tree in the courtyard, with her arms folded over her head.

"Enough whining! Forget the man who scratched your heart!" ordered Néhémie. "Get on one of those boats that cart black folk over to France! Your fortune awaits you there. FRANCE, I read that word written in big letters for you, a wide banner being paraded around in the middle of a fanfare. Here: the cemetery, over there: France-Deliverance."

Marga stood up as if she'd just had a glimpse of the Virgin Mary. Stuttering and casting out to the left and right bits of words and cries, she pulled up her skirts and ran toward the field where her papa was trimming the branches of a scraggly row of immortelle trees.

Her mission accomplished, Néhémie was already turning around when Clodomir's hoarse voice rose behind her.

"You always dream the truth, Néné," he said softly. "And you still ain't dreamt of me? Are you sure you don't regret nothing, Néné? It's been five years since my wife left me . . . Today you here to save my daughter, but don't you want me to save you, Néné? It ain't too late, you know. It ain't never too late for that . . ." She had laughed.

And now, on the day of her death, at ninety-five years of age, the words of that black man Clodomir came humming irritatingly around her ears. No, she wasn't dreaming. She could hear him and see him exactly as he was before: bold, happy to be a man set down on this earth. He was convinced she would grow bitter and remorseful with age. She saw him at age sixty-eight, handsome, wearing his black Dacron suit, a tie around his neck, eyes closed, hair combed, so peaceful and elegant in his varnished wooden coffin, wads of cotton stuck into all the orifices in his body.

And now—all because of Clodomir—at the end of her life when she lay down to await death, Néhémie felt the need for love and understood the meaning of regret for the very first time. Grim regret, thrashing and screaming, unleashed. Raging, spiteful regret, spitting its venom at the mealy-mouthed dreams preparing to aid her in the last hours of her life. Regret that seized and shook her, trampled her noble serenity into the ground. And the words that the man had sown long ago like seeds on rocky soil suddenly burst open, germinated wildly in her being, sprouting immense leaves and bouquets of flowers with garish scents, large red petals, like the bitter drooping mouths of women in search of men. Regret at not having lived at least one of the passionate mysteries of love that she had dreamt, unraveled, and shed light upon. Regret at having always kept her heart in a nice dry place. Regret at not having tasted the flesh of a single man, even if he'd been an insignificant good-for-nothing, a blind, deaf, crippled, emaciated wreck . . . And Clodomir's empoisoned words, heady and spicy smelling, came and planted themselves all around her, on the sheets and the pillowcase, masking the quiet dreams that were already beginning to fill the cabin. Then, on her deathbed, Néhémie called out to Clodomir. Faint-heartedly at first, with a voice that came from under the fronds of her virginity. "Clodomir! Clodomir!" until she felt him lying atop her, strong, warm, and brimming with the love that he had tried so many times to anchor in her heart.

Néhémie's last hour was filled with rapture; it was an apotheosis, a prelude to paradise. And her last breath wasn't the rail of a sinner vanquished by death, but the cry of a woman fulfilled, abandoning herself. None of the neighbors who came running to her side ever forgot Néhémie's transfigured face.

That is how Néhémie expired, not like she had lived, solitary and dreamy, but like the women on this earth who come so very near to death every day in the joining of bodies, only to be reborn with a taste of eternity on their tongue.

Her sole companion, an ageless, scrawny bird that she'd kept caged from the beginning of her first revelations, died of grief. For every morning, Néhémie had fed it on dreams. They even say that the bird shed a tear when they carried its old friend away. It soon lost its voice, stopped eating and drinking. One evening, the children of one of the neighbors who'd adopted the bird, found its little body dried up under its perch, wings folded, beak closed over a red rosebud.

Nobody wanted to touch the bird or open the cage. People examined it through the red-painted bars. Kept repeating the innocent words of a young black girl who asked, pointing to the red rosebud in the bird's beak, if that was really Dame Néhémie's heart.

Fearing that misfortune would fall upon the inhabitants of

Saint-Jean, two courageous young men carried the cage and the dead bird back to Néhémie's cabin at the end of a long pole.

No one asked many questions for quite some time. Every now and again, when folks stayed up late, certain lips would pronounce Néhémie's name, suggesting to everyone present that an expedition should be organized to verify that the heart was still locked inside the cage . . . They were met with silence. Then, a soft breeze would sweep their words away, rub the leaves of the trees up against one another until they began whispering stories of love between birds and flowers.

Years later, one of Néhémie's godsons, a military man stationed in Besançon, arrived from France with a surprise: a white woman. She was almost pink, with green eyes and yellow hair like a *chabine* from around our parts. Confronted with the *fait accompli,* his mother fainted and fell over backward on the wharf of Point-à-Pitre where the ocean liner *Mermoz* was at anchor. She cursed her son, threatened to disinherit him, and refused to put him up in her house. Charitable hands entrusted him with the keys to his godmother Néhémie's house. The couple spent their days on the beach. Went out without locking the doors to the cabin. That is how the cage, the dead bird, and the rosebud disappeared.

Most people who'd known Néhémie could only partially recall her passage on earth. They'd erased that last gasp and Clodomir's name from their minds, just as years before they had forgotten the blood-red flower stain that had bloomed on young Néhémie's dress the day of her Solemn Communion. Her last minutes were just like that deplorable mark: an accident of life. A stain as a reminder of human impurity that had to be dutifully buried along with the body in the grave so that only the immaculate image of the guardian of dreams would remain, the supreme and uncontested legatee that she had been all of her life.

Soon, survivors from those days only opened their mouths to describe in minute detail the glorious day of her funeral. Myriads of flowers framed her body. So many flowers carried by the armful to Dame Néhémie's bedside . . . No! Not a single person had broken their promise. Countless hands laid flowers in her coffin so that she would still smell good when she reached the other shore. Red ginger flowers. Bird-of-paradise flowers. Hibiscus and lavender. Creole rosebuds. Arums and wine-colored anthuriums. Violets, wild pansies, and corn poppies. Begonias . . . Tiny wildflowers from the fields, buttonweeds and innocents, picked in the very heat of day and already wilted. Flowers smelling of gratitude and grief mingling against their will with the unspeakable bright red, spicy, heady ones that Clodomir had sent to Néhémie's side first.

5

The story of Néhémie's funeral had often been related to Clothilde, her great-great-grandniece . . .

Clothilde, who was found lifeless beside Robert in 1961 in that room in Basse-Terre, had not known an ordinary childhood for very long. When her mother Gérémise noticed that her child had inherited Néhémie's power of interpretation, she immediately began treating her like a valuable asset locked up in a safe she carefully guarded. Mornings, while her two brothers ran out to tie up the oxen and the goats in the savannah, Clothilde was packing up the last of the night's dreams in her still sleepy mind.

The sunlight didn't simply fall upon her face; it sprinkled powdered gold over her. Her eyes—opened wide in her dreams—rolled under her closed eyelids. Her fingers limbered themselves up by drumming on the sheets. Her hands separated from her body and began to flap gracefully. When she finally awoke, she did not declare: "I dreamt this or that," but rather: "I was traveling beyond the world again!" She sat up on the edge of the bed, shook her head to bring order to the exact words that were to recount her dreams. Silence immediately reigned in the room. Then began the tale of her travels, the description of the lands traversed and the strangers whom she had glimpsed, battled, or come to the aid of. Her words flowed out at first in chiaroscuros, like a parable. And then came the pure moment of interpretation punctuated by words that even she had never heard and that sprang to her lips naked and lovely. She used them with perfect mastery and insolent clarity. Sometimes she even gabbled in English, Spanish, or Latin. And everyone, ecstatic before her extraordinary inheritance, gauged the immensity of that gift.

At the age of twelve, Clothilde was already very renowned in Saint-Jean. Most people had forgotten her first name and, in homage to Néhémie, would call out to her with sincere benevolence: "Ti Néné!" Her mother Gérémise believed the girl's future was all laid out for her, the only thing Clothilde needed to do was place her footsteps in those of her great aunt. Dreams were a benediction and money a sublime compensation.

Clients thronged around Ti Néné, dazzled and confident, jealous and dubious, to submit snatches of dreams to her that she dissected with phenomenal facility. Considering the interpretations to be divine assistance, they wanted to possess the keys to the future they had glimpsed in their slumber without being able to define it. They would come avidly forward, bristling with demands. Clothilde was to evaluate the exact amount of time that was left to them, the circumstances and the date of their death, the number of children to be born, the winning numbers of the national lottery, their lucky and unlucky days.

Many managed to squeeze out of her the name of the future husband, the name of their enemy, that of the dog that pursued them in a nightmare chase, the rank of the toad in dress uniform, starched shirt, silk tie, who strummed on a guitar on the black and white waters of a dream smelling of alkali.

Some, who were less excited, would whisper their tales into her ear, convinced they were to return home armed, prepared to ward off all blows, filled with wisdom they bore like a suit of bronze armor.

Impassioned ones would come running up, panting, their head allegedly filled with epic and flamboyant dreams that they had to tell without delay. But—empty gourds—they couldn't remember the nocturnal journeys. So then they would stammer out rantings and ravings or else gloomy melodramas shabbily patched together. In the end, they would always beg Clothilde to dream in their place and would go home singing-whistling, their hearts delighted, and their minds aglow with comical hope.

Another category mailed in descriptions of fantasies that Ti Néné speedily dusted off, sending her answer back the same day. She also counted amongst her clientele some very old, decrepit, toothless bodies who left at her doorstep the intolerable garments of wisdom and reason that, due to their great age, they were forced to don. They came to her like babes, innocent, lost, fragile, and vulnerable. The ones she called the pitiful, those who were the most disconcerted, begged for her science, listened to her with fervent religiosity, as if she held the power to bring them back to their youthful years, to add credit to their days and pull them out of time . . . At times like that, Ti Néné could feel herself floating above the world between heaven and earth. Neither dead nor alive. Evanescent.

Perhaps it was that feeling that caused Clothilde to become estranged from school. And perhaps even more so, the dreadful behavior of her schoolteachers, who had ended up coming to solicit her one after the other. Authoritative and proud, they would shoot off at her child's ears triangular or perpendicular dreams, dreams with multi-digit numbers, and other complexities that the pupil had to untangle on the spot for fear of being beaten and scolded in class over a small spelling error or a slip up on a grammar rule.

At fifteen, Clothilde was thought of as an oracle, and her fame had spread past the three bridges that linked Saint-Jean to the rest of the universe. She had already predicted the mayor's reelection twice, augured that General de Gaulle would take the reins of power back up again, and given the precise names, times, and dates of the next three cyclones. As a matter of fact, people did not speak of her like a flesh and blood person but rather like a monument cut out of stone. A sort of caryatid whose shoulders, neck, and head were strong enough to hold up more and more mountains of dreams. People in general and her mama Gérémise, in particular, thought of her as being entirely devoted—and for centuries to come—to poor sinners, the utter slave of the charge bequeathed by Néhémie. Dreams of glory, of riches, of hope, of health. She was the crossroads of their destiny, the only rock to which they might confidently moor their illusions. Dream in caraco or striped pants. Dream of goose feathers and blue blood. Tanned dream of deep waters. Dream of a man with a sun head and a woman with elephant feet. Dream of precipices and cliffs. Sapodilla and cocoa dream. Vomit and gold coins dream. Dream of crossing a sea, white ocean liner, square of madras. Our Father who art in heaven dream. Belzebuth and *soucougnans* dream. Dream big knife and barrels of pickled offal meat. Dream seven, twelve, thirteen, twenty-five hallelujah! Dream misplaced shoes and broken leg. Dream change purse found and *millefeuille* of bank notes . . . Dreams by the cartloads until nausea rises. Too wonderful dreams that derailed onto parallel routes. Never got back to the glum reality—closely approximated at times but fading away on the horizon of illusory happiness. Volatile and insubstantial, swaggering and petty dream. Dreams that presage marriages and funerals, outrages and criminals. Dreams in cascades. Dream in episodes. Stairsteps dream to go up and down. Jack of spades and queen of hearts dream . . .

In 1957, at the age of sixteen, Clothilde did not obtain her certificate attesting to the completion of her secondary education and gave up on school for good. Most of her schoolmates, condemned to working in the cane fields beside their mothers and fathers, were secretly jealous of the destiny that was so nicely cut out for her. And no one would have thought that in truth she was already fed up with living in dreams. Though Clothilde was subjected to the procession of people, she didn't go out with anyone, didn't have the slightest confidante, either friend or enemy. And even though she sometimes found pleasure in dream-telling, and in playing magician too, blowing on the dreams to loosen the tight knots, she had long wanted to step down from the pedestal she'd been stuck up on, get back at last to the world of the living where love curdled the blood, where laughter and tears straddled one another, where desire unfurled, swirled into a gale, filling the sail, only to quail, slink away, slippery serpent tail. The world in which the heart, a hundred times rejected and shattered, always healed anew, by some sort of miraculous chemistry that she wanted to feel in her own flesh, hold in her arms and kiss.

Thanks to her daughter's gifts, Gérémise had already had five houses built of concrete and wood that she rented in Grands-Fonds Sainte-Anne. Clothilde's consultations were of course free. However, the good Lord is good! Everyone who came to call on her left something, some ingratiating change, two-three gratifying bank notes, in a cup placed ostensibly on a console table in the entryway, near a wooden cross upon which the crucified Christ Our Lord, reminded the assembly of visitors of their condition as sinners, the required repentance, and the expected offering.

One morning when she was twenty, Clothilde told her mother Gérémise that she had read her own name on the first page of *La Quotidienne de la Guadeloupe* in a dream. She had seen herself popular and famous. She lived in the hills of Basse-Terre and invented perfumes.

"And the dreams?" enquired Gérémise. "And the dreams! Tell me, what about the dreams?"

Clothilde had been refusing to elucidate the slightest dream, narrate her enchanted journeys for a whole year now. She had turned away everyone who had developed a habit and a taste for listening to her interpretations. The folks felt as if they were falling apart in the face of her silence and her indifferent gaze. Bewildered, burdened with accumulated fantasies, they no longer knew how to lead their lives, go forward or backward, marry Paul or Justin, live a little longer or die at such and such a time, have a baby girl or boy, vote for this guy or that guy.

Gérémise had waited patiently and asked all the miserable people crowding at her door to do the same. She had refrained from shaking Clothilde in the hopes of bringing down a few dreams. She hadn't beaten her, had not thrown stones like one does at a tree that is holding back its ripe fruit. She had knelt down, prayed God to come to her aid, asked for three masses to be held for Néhémie's soul, and stuck candles on her grave.

From the time Clothilde was ten onward, the whole family had depended mainly on her. No one really worked anymore. One evening in 1951, they'd watched the father go out to sea in his dinghy. The next morning Gérémise had waited on the beach for his return. Two days later, she slipped on a black dress, lit candles, and laid out lambi conches in a cross on the beach. And that is how she became a widow at forty without ever seeing her husband's body again. Clothilde's two brothers had abandoned the fields and only exerted themselves on the first day of the month, when they collected the rent from the five houses built thanks to the generosity of dreamers who came flocking at all hours, and sometimes from great distances, to drink in Clothilde's good word. They each had a black Peugeot car, identical to the mayor's. The elder loved gambling, and the younger women. They collected the money all right, counted it, tucked it away in their leather billfolds. But it always ended up evaporating somehow and they didn't worry too much about it.

Gérémise prayed, took Communion, confessed before confiding her distress to three *gadézaffè*-conjurors. She never was able to understand the source of the problem or the reason the dreams had been interrupted. She feigned to accept not living amongst dreams any longer, not listening to the flow of Ti Néné's words, the marvelous source that enriched her life. But deep down inside, the idea that Great-aunt Néhémie had withdrawn from Clothilde never really took hold. Up until her daughter's death, she felt that her silence was a calamity.

When Clothilde came to relate her dream of love and celebrity, on the first page of *La Quotidienne de la Guadeloupe*, and that story about perfume, Gérémise thought she'd reached the end of her trials, the end of the lean times.

"And the dreams?" she asked Clothilde once again.

"I finished with the dreams, Mama . . . there ain't never going to be no more dreams. I want to discover the world and its beauties . . ."

Gérémise bit her lips, nodded her head, and looked out the window as if, all of a sudden, she could embrace the world of beauties Clothilde spoke of. She repeated softly, "The world, its beauties . . . And what you say about its ugliness, girl?"

Since she'd stopped dreaming, every morning Clothilde would walk out into the countryside barefoot, a basket on her head. She came back in the evening with loads of flowers. Even before seeing her in person, one was inebriated by the fragrances that preceded the girl. She spent the night decanting her harvest in bottles and vials for maceration, concentration, and distillation.

"There's always some beauty in the ugliness of the world, Mama. I seen its breath, its flavor, and its colors. I dreamt them. I going away to find life and its five senses. I dreamt love and celebrity. I'll write you . . ."

"And you leaving me just like that, Clothilde? You abandoning those who believe in you, girl . . . They got a right to know, and you got to serve them; it's your duty! You a saint, Clothilde . . ."

"No! Not a saint!"

"But they got a right!" insisted Gérémise.

Clothilde wiped a tear from her cheek.

"Before I go, I got to tell you one last thing, Mama. When my father disappeared at sea, I had a dream about it. And I never said nothing. I saw the wave sweep him away. I saw his body flailing about for a long time. I saw his hat floating on the surface of the water. I kept it all to myself, to see whether dreams really control life. Would he still be alive? Would he have gone out fishing that day if I'd told him about his overturned dinghy in the middle of the ocean? I didn't say nothing . . . And he died . . ."

Clothilde left Saint-Jean the day after that last revelation. At the big marketplace in Basse-Terre, she displayed her perfumes for sale amidst dried flowers, herbal teas, and bitter roots. Rented a little room not far from the prefecture building. And eked out her life there with the meager earnings from her business. Then no one heard much about her except through the sailors, the dockers, and fishermen—blacks and whites from the Saints—who hung around the wharf. She sold her body for a modest sum, swore the men who'd never run into such a beauty on the wharves of Basse-Terre. Always strongly perfumed, she gave herself passionately to all and sundry, seeking true love in every embrace, in every glance, in the slightest awkward and calloused caress of those large-handed men. As a goodbye—and that was what gradually softened the hearts of her conquests—she would offer them flowers after their close quarter combat. And they left feeling warmed and deeply stirred by that gentle whore, a bit inebriated and nauseous, as if they had mistakenly lifted the skirts of the Blessed Virgin or else happened upon their own mother in the nude. They assumed that she must surely have ended up there due to some sort of unnatural doings, a diabolical pact or an ancestral sin, but they couldn't resist the attraction they felt for her. Though they sometimes feared perishing in her arms or else chaining their destiny to her ill-fated one, they abandoned themselves to her, scrounged for a bit of love, a taste of fulfillment, and tried to see themselves as gods, immortal and blissful, for the space of an animal-like grunt and an exquisite sigh. In their company, Clothilde was under the impression that she came very close to love, very close to dying once and for all, but she would always come back to life, lift herself from her ecstasy feeling as if she'd been sullied. Those men drew cries, moans, whimpers from her—but the love she was waiting for would not blossom. It seemed to be everywhere and nowhere, crouching behind promises of happiness and delightful kisses, locked away under velvet eyes and satan caresses, curling up between satin soft words. Always just within hand's reach, always invited and never requited.

Robert, Sybille's father, had grudgingly gone into town to buy some blood sausage for Noémie, his young wife, pregnant with their second child. It was a Monday, a fast day. Drawn from one place to the next by unknown friends posted on the street corners just so that his destiny might be fulfilled, he had related, at each station, the frantic craving for blood sausage that had taken hold of Noémie. He'd been guided to Camilla's paved alley. The mulatto woman, it was claimed, sold tripe, pickled pigs' feet, and snouts at her doorstep every single day of the week. The old woman listened to his story. Disappeared. Came back empty-handed. Looked him up and down and questioned him about his family and trade. Went off to rummage around amongst some pots in a sort of lean-to. Then suggested he wait for an hour, the time it would take to prepare a string of blood sausage. Her nails were grimy, her eyes rheumy, but Robert promised to come back. His family! His trade! What a snoop, that woman! All that for a measly kilogram of blood sausage that she'd get God only knows where . . . he thought. Did the money he was going to shell out to her have a color, was it dirtier than the water she cooked the blood sausage in?

Robert went into the alley grumbling, talking to himself, thinking of his eight years of marriage with Noémie, who had already given him a pretty little Sybille. Dear Noémie who had never expressed the need for the smallest little thing, except to satisfy him in every way. Didn't ask for anything, not even a pair of sandals when the fishing was good and there were holes in her shoes. She almost always stood up tall and proud. And then that frantic craving for blood sausage had gripped her so intensely that for a moment he'd thought she might have been struck by one of those illnesses of the head that suddenly swoop down—no one knows how—that never really go away and that they try to cure at the Saint-Claude Asylum.

One day when the aversion he felt for fishing had gotten a firmer grip on him than usual, he'd gone over there to ask for a job as a gardener. What he saw there had remained locked in his mind, had overwhelmed him, and, for a long time, filled him with fear that he might have been contaminated by one of the insane or carried out, on the heels of his shoes, part of the madness concentrated in there. Strong men walking on their hands and knees, toothless, giggling, and terrifying. Women, hair tousled, lifting up their skirts as he passed and shaking their flaccid buttocks and their woolly *coucounes* before the blank-eyed drove of pitiful geezers, escaped from a dark world, rocking, endlessly rocking. Fearsome visages, horrifying bodies, arms and legs hastily shaped by vile nature. Unfounded cries of joy. Cries of fear. Terror in the face of invisible blows, of intangible devils, repulsive satans. Cries, "Help, Lord God! Save me from the demons that are trying to kill me! Help! Lord God, I implore You!

Deliver me from the evil hordes that are ripping my soul apart!" Rasping cries. Haunting, heartbreaking cries. Strings of cries drifting up from beyond the grave, from other ages, from beyond the sea. Cries from the brink of death. And their eyes! So many eyes fixed upon him, drifting in distraught faces, blinking in the dungeon-like darkness traversed by ephemeral flickers of light. Glowing eyes behind drooping and creased eyelids. Eyes broken into thirteen splinters, crushed under the weight of recurring sorrow, faded from the wash of inner tears as powerful as rogue waves. Yellowed eyes, like old incurable puss-filled wounds.

To rid himself of those insane thoughts and not mix Noémie up with the souls gathered and exiled at the asylum, tossed about on the ocean like a lost ship, with neither tiller nor captain, he decided to go call on Edgar, his father's brother, whom he hadn't seen since his marriage. In the meantime, Camilla would have plenty of time to prepare the blood sausage, he told himself.

After his visit to the asylum, Robert had given up on his brief vocation to be a gardener and fell back on fishing, as one might consent to a marriage of convenience. Without loving the trade, he respected it all the same, just as all the men in his family for the last three generations had.

His old uncle lived two streets farther away. Robert would take the opportunity to remind him that he was still ready to buy the dinghy they had haggled over several times. Rather than sell it, his uncle—who'd retired three years earlier—was letting the boat rot under pieces of sheetmetal, which he called a hangar.

Alas, Edgar had gone out into his fields. The cabin was closed and the dinghy filled with empty bottles and dirty oil cans. Annoyed, Robert walked down the street and went back to see Camilla who handed him an armful of steaming black blood sausage. He threw her money down and returned neither her smile nor her good-bye.

On his way home, he passed Clothilde and started walking behind her, stupidly, as one follows an idea without beginning or end. An idea that springs up from who knows where, fills the head, then arouses the senses, and devours the soul. He didn't follow her on account of her half-bare legs or her rhythmic stride proclaiming at every step: "Take me from the left! Take me from the right! Take me from the front! Take me from behind!" but because of her smell. That particular day, Clothilde had rubbed her body with a mixture of ground ilang-ilang flowers, vanilla pods, nutmeg, as well as mint and basil leaves. All of the fragrances, each in turn, stood out distinctly from one another, suddenly becoming either more pronounced or fading away after rounding the corner of a cabin, struggling to dominate one another and above all to quell the fabulous effluviums exuding from Clothilde. In truth he was following her like a dog in the wake of its mistress, heart pounding, chops hanging slack and drooling, nostrils quivering at those generous effusions that lent—it was glaringly obvious—flesh and consistency to the word *love*.

He had gone out with a few donzellas before marrying Noémie. He even had a daughter, Louise, whom he hardly knew. Like all men, he had been enticed by bottoms, lips, and eyes. Since his marriage, he'd already strayed a few times, answering—in spite of himself—the call of frantic thrusts of the pelvis, sustained smiles, I-believe-in-you looks. But he had repented, promising himself not to succumb to the sins of the flesh again, to resist the heartaches-headaches, the attractions-malefactions, and the intercourse-remorse. Robert wasn't a womanizer, just an ordinary fellar who, without knowledge or foreknowledge, was at the mercy of life's pitfalls, ripped and torn between the legion of upright thoughts and the malevolent army of angels of evil that always spurred one on to the worst, encouraged vile instincts, predicted paradises, star-studded heavens, and life by the shipload with theatrical laughter and gaudy words that glittered brighter than all the gold teeth lining their gums. Burned several times, Robert had managed to come through with only a few scratches, wounds from the battle of love. And though Noémie had gotten wind of two-three of his tumbles, she'd forgiven the man and bore him no grudges, which is the custom in our parts. What use would it have been, since he'd come back each time, though febrile, tongue a bit furred from having betrayed, and heart seesawing between male pride and guilt.

It had been a good year that he hadn't gone running after new creatures. His marriage with Noémie seemed to be anchored in the peacefulness of calm waters. He even believed he'd already entered into another realm of the sphere, where demon tempters of the flesh no longer prowled. He wasn't seeking a woman, he'd just gone into town to satisfy Noémie's craving for blood sausage.

The night before, Clothilde had dreamt that one of her perfumes would bring her the love she had so long desired. All she had to do was walk out her cabin door. Knowing what awaited her, she had thus readied herself serenely, as one would await a well-earned salary. She had stuck three tulips from Senegal into her hair and was holding a red rosebud in her hand.

Ever since she'd been sharing her body with the men on the wharf of Basse-Terre, Clothilde had never ceased thinking of her father whom she'd been unable to keep alive. I dreamt his death, she repeated to herself every day. I watched him thrash around in the middle of the sea, and paddle with both hands and bail water, and pray God to come to his aid. I watched it, and I said nothing when he gathered up his pots and nets the next day, promised a catch of pink and white fish.

Sometimes the gestures of lovemaking that she invented with the men from the wharves in Basse-Terre changed into acts of lifesaving. Seven times, yes, seven, she'd felt as if she were holding a drowned man in her arms. First the man would flail around. And then gasp for air, panting tragically. His eyes would turn white. His limbs would stiffen. All of a sudden he would sink into death. So then Clothilde's body became a buoy, a raft, a dinghy, a ship. Her arms and legs became a main mast, oars, and a sail. She put all her breath into it and brought the man back to life at the risk of losing her own. Seven, she had saved seven of them.

She knew immediately that Robert was a fisherman. From the smell of shellfish about him. From his slightly swaying gait. From his broad galley-slave shoulders. From the way he held his head, and from his eyes that were constantly rolling round, seeking and singling out invisible points of reference between the sky, the land, and the sea. She recognized him above all by his heart, which did not beat any faster than that of ordinary people, but spoke to hers without detour, with words of sand and saltwater. Coral-words of mother-of-pearl and fish scales. Drifting navy blue words.

One behind the other, they walked along in that fashion for a long time. She, stepping firmly out in front of her slowly shrinking shadow, turning around from time to time to offer him her gaze, her soul to listen to, and send him perfumed kisses that flew over to him, encircled him, then settled upon his lips, flowed down the length of his neck, crept into his hair. Such mad, such sweet kisses that he got goose bumps. He, taking longer strides, making as if to catch up to her, to hold her back, to lose her . . . Delaying the moment he would touch her flesh for real, first just the tips of her fingers, her feet, her thighs . . . Deferring the instant in which he would bury his nose in her armpits and his tongue in her mouth.

When she climbed the little *morne* that led to her room, Robert was suffocating. Clothilde heard him breathing heavily, but she didn't turn around for fear he would be wearing the mask of those drowned men she'd already saved.

"Robert, it's time you got your feet out of this craft!" an inner voice advised him. "You can still save your body. There are several holes in the bark. Flee this place of perdition! . . . Come back to your senses, Robert! Noémie is awaiting your return . . . You promised her. You promised . . ."

But already, Robert had stopped listening. Inebriated, suddenly deprived of all reason, he simply shooed away the wise words that were knocking around inside of him like huge blind June bugs.

In spite of the half-light, he walked into the room, bowing his head just enough to avoid the low wooden beams. He walked over to the large bed as if he were in a familiar place. There, without taking off his shoes, he lay down on the flowered bedspread and contemplated in wonder the timbers where a multitude of bouquets with faded colors hung upside-down endlessly drying. He was smiling, the poor devil, while behind their withered petals, those thousands of bitter creatures were secretly spying on him, like soured women who had never discovered love. So many Néhémies come to the end of their lives. Mortified, their hearts reduced to a snipped rosebud, wilted before even having known what blossoming was. And sad, faces livid, filled with regrets, refusing to leave this world, clinging with all their claws, with all their thorny thoughts to this terrestrial life filled with delights and with torments.

The room was a sort of mausoleum, with the bed set smack in the middle, upon which the long, confident body of that fool Robert was awaiting love. He had abandoned himself to the red petals of the new bedspread. He was blissfully admiring the sky of dried flowers and the rows of brown tapers that Ti Néné made herself light, one after the other, getting her feet caught in the spider webs that fizzled, giving off an unpleasant odor of burnt hair.

Clothilde took off her dress. Robert closed his eyes. He thought for a moment of Noémie disfigured by her craving for blood sausage. Then various thoughts beset him. Three children appeared: Louise, his first daughter whom he had had with Roselaine, a young Indian woman from Saint-François, in the days when, as a single man, he was finishing up his military service . . . Sybille, in tears, staggering, holding a dead baby in her arms, whom she stared at lovingly and called her little brother . . . Behind them, her mother, sitting naked on a boulder. Her heavy breasts hanging down on her stomach. Without making the slightest effort to cover her nudity, she was fixing her grey, tousled hair, making thousands of parts on her head. Looking worried, she lifted her nose from time to time to watch the dark sky . . . His uncle, lying in his dinghy as if in a coffin, drifting off toward cruel seas . . . And then, the old concoctress of Monday blood sausage sprang up out of the shadows, making wild gestures before disappearing . . .

When he opened his eyes, Robert caught Clothilde rummaging in a dresser drawer, where small, carefully labeled vials containing perfumes she had made were dubbed: "Enchanted Romance," "Blissful Longing," "Transported," "Love's Melody,"

"Flaming Heart," and even "Dark Fever," "Pink Torment," "Mad Kiss," "Dream Come True," "Servitude," "Fidelity," "Passionately" . . . She chose one, never worn before, that she was saving for the big day of Love. "Miraculous Catch" was a skillful mixture of sea waters, true tears, and oil from a coconut found on Roseau Beach. She poured the contents of the bottle onto her head, rubbed her face, arms, and legs with it. Tied a fine white ribbon around her neck. Lastly, grabbed a metal cage that had once been painted red, but that rust must have begun attacking long before her birth.

The cage, which ended up there no one knows how, still held Néhémie's little dried up dead bird in it. It was so shrunken it could have fit in a child's closed fist. Clothilde pushed the bird away and delicately picked up the red rosebud. She lay down on Robert's chest to listen to his heartbeat, get drunk on its melodies. But she heard the sea like in a seashell. Then, the galloping of a horse. Finally the steps of love moving gradually closer. She heard voices coming from elsewhere. Laughter and crying. That was when the rosebud quivered, then throbbed, and the petals opened out, one after the other.

Lying atop Clothilde, Robert smiled at life's tossing about on the waters of chance, just like at sea. At life and at love unfurling furiously, dismasting destinies. He forgot Noémie, the child she was expecting. Forgot the old mulatto woman with black curved nails who cooked up blood sausage on Mondays. Forgot the asylum and its frightening creatures. There was nothing left but Clothilde and her perfumes that had already sunk so many men. Clothilde infused with the vehement certainty of having at last encountered love and not some poor drifter, cast about from wave to wave . . . Some ordinary drowned man's zombie, flesh ripped apart by the teeth of a shark, eyes devoured by small voracious fishes, head covered with seashells . . . Some poor soul washed up on the beach, spit out by the sea, given back to the land. This time, she had a live fisherman in her bed, a man of salt and water, a figurehead of love . . .

• • •

Pensive, alone in her room, folding clothes into her suitcases, Sybille was talking to herself, piecing together the memories of Guadeloupe that were crowding her thoughts.

"Now I'm doing exactly what you used to," she whispered at the portrait of her old friend Lila that she'd hung on the wall.

I was seven when it happened. My papa Robert and that Clothilde, nicknamed Ti Néné, discovered dead on a bed, in a cabin in the hills of Basse-Terre. The friends who came to visit Judes and Coraline always believed they spoke of it in my presence with lowered voices, in order to spare my young heart and preserve my soul. But I clearly remembered that morning when the craving for blood sausage had taken hold of my mother Noémie. Jaws clenched, she was holding up her huge belly between her hands. Long before that day, women had announced sometimes a girl, sometimes a boy, depending on the moon and the roundness of her silhouette. She would laugh at each prediction.

On that morning, she had asked, "Robert, what you got to say about it?"

He'd shrugged his shoulders. In the time it took him to turn around, doubled over, seized with a yearning for blood sausage, Noémie was licking her lips. Pig blood sausage, hot, greasy, shiny.

"Wait till Saturday," my papa answered.

"I want some right now. Not Saturday! Right this minute!"

"Why you getting vexed like that? You'll eat blood sausage next Saturday. Old man Toto's killing a pig!"

"You the one want to kill me! Today Monday! Lord, save me!"

"Now what you talking about, Nono! What's got into you? Today Monday, you not going to find blood sausage anywhere!"

"I can't wait for Saturday, Robert!" And she'd suddenly fallen over on her back, yelling, kicking her feet, stuffing earth into her mouth! "Blood sausage! I want blood sausage!"

Teeth covered with dirt, she demanded blood sausage, spitting out black mud . . . "Blood sausage! Blood sausage, Robert! I want it so bad . . ." And then she'd suddenly fallen silent. Her long black arms had started rocking her belly faster. Her dress was hiked up on her thighs. She looked at me as if she were preparing to die, right there before my eyes.

That morning, after my father Robert had left, she pulled me over to her in order to kiss me with her pointed mouth full of dirt. Hard pecks of the beak.

It wasn't the first time I'd seen my mother Noémie act like that. But that day, I was truly afraid of that Noémie who was my mama.

I remember her silence. Her face slowly grimacing as the words that were cudgeling home the death of my papa Robert, became authentic, definitive, and degenerated into nightmares. After a while, Noémie had turned everyone away. We were alone.

I remember: her belly had started forming humps, living, terrifying humps.

I remember: she just stood there in a pool of blood.

I remember her being dazed when the baby came out. She never cried out. Looked at it . . . For a long time . . . Dangling between her thighs. Upside down. Strangled by the umbilical cord. It was a boy. He didn't survive. After the two funerals, when I was nine years old, my mama Noémie took me to Pointe-à-Pitre to see Judes and Coraline, for whom she'd worked before her marriage. She dropped me off there, proud, dignified, and crazy from head to toe. Later, she had to be taken to the Saint-Claude Asylum where she passed away without ever understanding what had caused her life to collapse in that way.

6

Sometimes Lila would stop what she was getting ready to do or say. Suddenly, she could no longer hear the sounds of reality. Would open the curtains and look out the window leaning on her elbow as if, on the roof of the building across the street, people had called to her. Lila would remain like that for a long time, eyes squinting up little by little. Would wait for her head in her hand to weigh three centuries and for the television antennas and the electric wires to begin vibrating, be transformed into living beings straight out of her past, zombies escaped from the red brick and the black chimneys. She forced herself to sink into those visions. To set the scene. Making her mind animate the brick, the metal, and the plastic. It did her both good and caused her pain at the same time. It made her blood run cold and her lower abdomen feel queasy. At those times she couldn't care less that the sun wasn't smack dab in the middle of the sky, couldn't care less that the clouds swelled her head up with ashes or that the frost embroidered lacy patterns on the window panes. She would watch the buses and trains passing by, and the people moving along on the electric wires. Walking. And then falling. Tripping. And falling one after the other, because of the suitcases that were too heavy, hurriedly packed, containing their entire lives, prayer books, and also retouched photographs of their old parents with carefully arranged hairdos. Grandfathers with dyed hair who smiled on command with hands folded. The men carried small brown and black pasteboard attaché cases holding only what was strictly necessary: tooth brushes, blue-striped pajamas, carefully pressed stiff collar shirts, ties, grey socks, and property titles to reclaim their possessions after the war . . .

Behind them, wives and mothers wearing long black coats in spite of the summer, platform shoes, and veiled hats under which pins were slipping out and buns were coming unraveled. Their eyelids were drooping for they were calculating the extent of the emptiness, the dizziness, and the terror more quickly than the men. Even though those women had gauged the precipices, they stepped up, boarded the freight cars. They moved forward, being already aware there would be no return. Somewhere, deep in their hearts, a small voice whispered that they would never come back to their cozy apartments. Would never dust off their porcelain knick-knacks again, never again pat the folded sheets in the wardrobes perfumed with lavender. Never again would their eyes count the treble stitches on their starched prewar crochet doilies, laid out on the end tables, the dining room table, the mantle. At times they thought of their sweet little caged birds condemned to die of hunger and loneliness. They thought of their plants deprived of water, of sunlight, and of love: geraniums, thujas, and rhododendrons that had grown in their living rooms and that would slowly wilt. They recalled themselves sitting and sewing yellow stars on the black wool of their coats.

Stars that came neither from the sky nor the sea.
Stars with five points cut with quick scissor slashes
from cheap cloth
Run through with the needle and thread.
Pressed with a hot iron onto the front of the coats.

The women had complied with the new laws, had obeyed all the orders they had been given. They lifted one foot after the other, making themselves walk at a steady pace, past the armed men looking on, as if they already knew where they were going. Without trembling, like automatons, they instinctively carried out maternal gestures: took firm hold of the children's hands so they wouldn't jump out in front of a car, knotted scarves to avoid colds, tied up loose shoelaces to prevent falls . . .

It was a winter day in the summer of 1942.

Children, Sybille! So many innocent children boarded those buses and trains . . .

The women were moving around on the roof of the building. And watching them in their extremely composed serenity, Lila always hoped that at the last minute, just before falling, wings would sprout from their backs, because after all there was a God to come to the aid of unfortunate souls who had reached the very end of their rope. There was an all-powerful God that those women invoked. He could create a path in the middle of the sea, change the river water into blood, orchestrate a deluge . . .

They were walking behind the men on the electric wires thinking of Moses and his people, so as not to feel the icy wind of the void on their necks and faces. And when they fell, their mouths remained open. A mute scream that didn't pierce Lila's ears, but burned her eyes that began to shine and fill up with tears. And for a long time, a very long time afterwards, her heart would jump at the dull sound of bodies hitting the bottom.

What Lila described wasn't exactly fresh. According to her, it smelled of rotten eggs, putrid wafts of decomposed flesh, of burnt hair and nails. Foul smells from an abominable past that stunk up the rooms, hung vile stars on the ceiling, and permeated the curtains with a stench even more tenacious than rank tobacco. Lila shook her limp blond permanent curls. Opened the windows up wide. And cursed, "Shit, Sybille, one of these days they're bound to leave me in peace!"

Her screams had the power of sending those creatures back to their shadows. Suddenly arms and legs tangled in tragic positions atop the buildings took on the appearance of metal antennas again. And the electric wires turned back into perching places for Parisian pigeons. When I would ask her who those people were, Lila would fly off the handle and glare at me as if I too were part of the nightmare. "You know very well who they are, Billy!" she grumbled, "You know . . ."

Those phantoms sometimes popped back up on the television, in old war films. Lila couldn't stand those pictures. She ordered Marcello to change the channel immediately. "May the dead be left with the dead! All of that is ancient history! Why in God's name do they want to stir up those days? Put Drucker on for us, Son!"

One evening when she'd had too much Johnny Walker to drink, Lila couldn't help herself, she started coming out with it, hidden behind the smoke from her Chesterfields. It was before we left for the States. Long before she started becoming obsessed with Henry. She was itching to get it out. But I wasn't to ask her any questions. Just listen to her, pass her the ash tray, and serve her whiskey when she held out her glass.

"They were up over my head. Right where you and your son Marcello are today. They came to get them. They were dragging their feet going down the stairs. One of them had tried to resist. So he'd been hit on the head. He was half unconscious. The others were holding him up. From my window, I saw them get on a bus. That's how they disappeared from my life. How they toppled over into the void. After that, oh, years later, I recognized them on the television. It might not really have been them. But people who looked so much like them, who were walking around with the same stars, the same black coats, the same suitcases, and who were getting onto buses and trains.

"They were polite people. When I passed them in the hallway, the men would take off their hats. The women would pull the children against their thighs. One of them was pregnant. They couldn't have been more discreet. We never heard a sound from them. Not even the children, Sybille. And there were children all right. Three children and some caged birds . . ."

All of a sudden, Lila was completely sucked into the echoes of the period of her life she had been trying to flee for fifty years. She spoke as if the words were being dictated to her. Heaving them up in the same way that she seemed to be nauseated with herself for having been a witness to that tragedy, powerless, an aider and abettor, and perhaps even at fault. The sentences were broken, faltering, scattered about like so many miserable cadavers. But the words, bit by bit, ended up nonetheless reconstituting the tragedy and the silhouettes of the people from the past, lending sound to the mute screams of women and children who had, one after the other, been swallowed up in the void.

Three children. There had been three children, four women, one of whom was pregnant. Five men. It was in 1942. They had been surviving for nine months in the two-room apartment directly above Lila's. Never opening the window. Going out during authorized hours. Hugging the walls to go and stand on the sidewalks, in the lines, in front of the deserted stands of the grocers who would accept money and ration tickets from people wearing yellow stars in exchange for some dry bread or some lard. Nine months, they had remained packed in there one against the other for nine months, like inside a mother's warm body. One couldn't even imagine the sleeping arrangements or how they managed with the bathroom and the need for privacy . . . How had the man and the woman about to give birth been able to forget the people all around, the yellow stars on the black coats, the parade of boots on the pavement of Paris, the ration cards . . . ? How had the man been able to overcome his fear, force his way through the thickets filled with evil shadows and penetrate so far, plant a seed of life in that woman's belly, when it was so cold all around, so cold in his heart?

Three children with emaciated faces, turned old and gray from having sucked on shame's milk and then having grown up in the war qualified with the terms Second and World, instead of ignoble and heinous. They were wearing coats whose sleeves were too short, that were too tight around their shoulders. Coats upon which mother's hands had sewn yellow stars.

Three children . . .

It was in July of 1942 . . .

Lila repeated the same snatches of sentences several times. Tramped into the paths of her memories. Kept seeing those poor people get onto the bus on the way to nowhere. Far away into the unimaginable, along a line of no return that ran down foggy corridors, flew over half-devastated bridges, wound through the unspeakable. A line drawn taught between what her memory had indelibly stamped into her and the black and white snapshots she had saved, old documentaries of war and the testimonies of survivors from the camps.

"First of all, Sybille, there had been thumping on the door. And suddenly a scuffle overhead. A commotion of overturned tables and chairs, the cries of women and children. And clusters of words that came springing out of the mayhem, 'No! No! Leave us alone!' And then the time it took to fill up the suitcases, the cavalcade on the stairs. I cracked open my door. I noticed their faces. 'Mercy! Oh have mercy on the children!' begged one woman clinging to the sleeve of a man in uniform. I watched them go down, Sybille. All of them . . . The ones who were dragging their feet. Those who were being pushed around. The man who was being held up by his friends. Those who walked along holding their heads high with the yellow star pinned to their jacket like a flower in a buttonhole. They were the ones who already knew that soon they would have nothing left, nothing but that dignity, which no one could take from them . . . Honor and the limited freedom of being able to look your executioner in the eye. Sybille, I saw the children's hands in those of their mothers. The pregnant woman's belly in her folded arms. A procession of yellow stars marching toward an already crowded bus. It was much later that someone spoke to me of Vel' d'hiv and the Drancy internment camp . . .

"After the war, as long as the apartment over my head remained unoccupied, I could hear them, Billy. All of them, the men, the women, and the children. They'd come back. Now you understand why I never wanted to rent it. It was their place up there. The war was over. They got together to laugh and dance, drink, smoke, live it up. Make the most of the things that help you forget what life on this earth is. They no longer had to hide, whisper, walk around in stocking feet. They would sing at the top of their lungs and drink until they passed out . . .

"I can't even count the number of people who came to ask about that two-room apartment. It remained unrented for thirty years. When I went up there to air it out, get rid of the mice, and shake out the carpets, nothing stirred. No music, not a trace of a ghost, or the last couplet of a caged bird. They had their periods. At times they wouldn't move so much as a toe for months. Then they would wake up, would shake each other. At first I could hear the laughter of the children. Clear laughter that rang out amongst the songs . . . I know the music, but I can't recall the words anymore. Wait a minute, it goes like this, Lalala la la la . . . And the birds would whistle the same tune . . . And then there would be marbles rolling on the floor boards. And the children would start to yell, cry, bicker, and swear, like all kids do, and run after one another through the rooms. And the men would start drinking, talking about love till they made the women's heads swim and then drag them into extravagant farandoles that lasted all night long. There was nothing left but dancing, loving, and living. You can picture that, Billy . . ."

That evening she kept me up quite late.

"Don't leave me, Billy! Look! Can't you see them? Look closer! In front of you, look where I'm pointing!"

I wiped the window clean with the scarf she was holding out to me. I opened my eyes wide to at least once catch a glimpse in the light of the lamppost of shapes other than chimneys, electric wires, and television antennas on the roof of the building across the street.

"Is it really true that you've never run into them, Billy? You've never heard them? So that's it; they only show up for me . . . Twelve yellow stars that don't want to go up to heaven . . ."

She laughed, coughed, and licked the dry corners of her mouth.

"So they really think I had something to do with their arrest . . . Look, Billy! They're sitting up on top of the building! They're watching us . . .

"Three children, I'm not exactly a monster . . .

"They were French. I'll swear to that. Not Germans, Billy! No, it's impossible that Hans could be mixed up in their arrest . . ."

Her eyes suddenly gleamed as the past came flooding into her living room, with all the colors of love, all the upheaval and the leaping of the heart, the mad acts, the heady smell, the burn of bodies.

"Hans! But Lila, I thought Henry . . ."

"Oh yes! Henry was also my love. Henry was quite special. You'll understand, he's a gem of a man, that Henry . . . But he came after Hans who had disappeared since August 20, 1943 . . . Don't be disappointed, Billy! It's not a sin to love several men in a lifetime!"

She laughed.

"Henry . . . If you'd known him back in the days when he wore his French army uniform! Yes, we were in love! He always knew Hans had come before him. For a long time I waited for a letter from Germany. Hans stepped out of my life just as he'd come in. And you see, Sybille, back when we were going out together, I was ashamed at times! I imagined people might denounce me to the resistance, tell them I was knocking around with a soldier from the German army. But I was in love and that was the only thing that mattered, that and the things we used to say to each other . . . After the war this . . . After the war that . . . We'll get married. We'll found a family, children, and that's not the half of it . . .

"Henry helped me get over Hans . . . You're going to get to know the man, the spitting image of a black American actor whose name I've forgotten. . . ."

There was already a lighthearted tone to her voice. As if, in spite of her chattering, her travel plans, her enthusiasm, she was aware that her path on this earth was growing shorter. She was already observing everything from the other shore. Her true self was showing through, free from anxiety, rid of torments, looking her phantoms straight in the eye.

At the same time as she was picturing Hans's tall silhouette, she felt glad she'd known so many lovers. At times she'd felt ashamed upon finding that German army jacket thrown over the back of a chair in the dining room. Ashamed when she saw the German boots set down at the foot of her bed. Ashamed at closing the door after him. So much shame mixed up with passion. So many "After the war" exchanges . . . "After the war, everything will be different, Lila" . . . "After the war, we'll get married, Hans" . . . "After the war, we'll travel . . ."

And while she was thinking about the way they used to embrace, like two children chilled to the very bone, spending hours decrypting the tender and promising messages in each other's eyes, Lila smiled and thanked her memory for faithfully restituting the moments of love she'd shared in her body and in her breast.

"The men that have crossed my path . . . There are some I've forgotten the names of today. Brutes! Losers, Billy! Real losers! But go figure why a woman gets undressed . . . Sometimes—you won't believe it—I did it out of pity, so that some poor dude wouldn't feel any dumber than the next. At times, I dreamt of Gabin while the man that was climbing up on me thought I was dying of desire for him. I didn't tell them, of course!

"I swear, I didn't chase after Hans. During that war, you know, there were people who spat on the German uniform. Who loathed everything about Germans as a whole . . . Hitler, the army, the SS, the Gestapo, they rolled everything up into one. And then there were those who listened to de Gaulle on *Radio Londres,* who fought behind the scenes . . . The world of the theater was a bit dubious. We were artists . . . And so, in the name of Art, there were some people who sold their souls for a paying role . . . But there were also love stories . . .

"The one with Hans . . .

"You'll say it sounds like sentimental nonsense, *Nous Deux* photo-novels, mushiness, whatever you like. There aren't enough words for love stories . . . Hans, he was sitting at the terrace of the Flore. Our eyes met. You know, Billy, you have to believe there are things that happen between human beings that there are no names for. Vibrations that have never been measured. It's like a sixth sense, do you understand that, Billy? A sixth sense that is only awakened when you run into the person you were meant to encounter at that particular time in your life.

"We didn't even need to talk. We recognized each other. And then the only thing left to do was give ourselves to one another.

"I don't want to think that he had anything to do with the

arrest of the poor people who lived on the floor above me. But after he left, the phantoms never let me be . . .

"It was the same with Henry. He had his own phantoms, back there in the West Indies. His mother Jenny, his white father whom he'd never been able to call daddy, and his fake father, the sad groom Michael, Jenny's fiancé, who hung himself rather than continue living in grief.

"Henry came and set anchor in my life with his ardent soul, his long hands full of caresses."

I had dreams for the night. So I got up. I drew the curtain on the stars that, perched on the roof of the building across the street, disturbed Lila. I had to start my shift at six the next morning. I was thinking about my patients, the injections, and the blood tests, my supervisor at La Salpêtrière who would not tolerate the slightest tardiness. I was picturing Marcello in Guadeloupe, with Judes and Coraline.

"Wait, Billy! Don't go!" Lila was reeking of whiskey and tobacco.

"Listen, I'm going to tell you one last thing that you don't know; it's that, as soon as I saw you, I understood that you would get that apartment. Oh my! You had a mouthful of words, one hell of a pitch. I just let you talk because you reminded me of Henry right away. The way you slip over the *rrr*'s. And then, above all, you had Marcello on your shoulder, and I just couldn't resist you. When I saw the two of you, I knew the phantoms would leave you be. I would have bet my life on that . . . And yet, you weren't the first black person to ask me for the apartment. But there was your baby . . . You showed up in 1976, if my memory serves me well . . .

"Because of Marcello . . . It's because of him too that we have to go to America to see Henry, eh, Sybille? Promise me!"

7

It's true, Lila had taken Marcello into her arms immediately, had pressed him close against her breast. She'd rubbed her powdered cheeks against Marcello's cold and pudgy ones, had stroked his hair and hands. He'd watched her without laughing, with the astonished look of someone who finds himself suddenly recognized by a friend who had taken no notice of him for a long time. And she had wept. He'd just turned one and he'd just met his second mother.

Sixteen years later, Marcello left us to go to Guadeloupe. And there we were alone, like two women deserted by the same man. Then Lila had started opening up her secret drawers, thinking about going to see Henry in America. Marcello was seventeen years old. It's silly to say, but he was still our little Lolo. Even if we knew very well we would never be strong enough to carry him like a baby, we hadn't noticed him growing up. I was sometimes astounded at his long limbs, which seemed enormous to me. His long hands resting on the table. His tapered fingers holding a teaspoon, his giant hairy legs sticking out of a pair of shorts, his enormous feet that took size 12 shoes . . . And Lila's presents! Clothes that were always too tight, toys for toddlers that he glared at scornfully . . . We barely noticed that he bent over to offer us his cheek.

He didn't even want us to take him to the Orly Airport. We embarrassed him. Lila had held him back by the sleeve of his jacket and kissed him at least ten times imploring him to take good care of himself, to come back very quickly. He dryly pulled himself loose. That was when I realized I hadn't seen his naked body since he was fourteen. Suddenly, I saw him in his entirety, gigantic, a man exactly like his papa Gino, in a hurry to break away from a woman, trapped by effusive displays of love. As he was going through the police checks, Lila called out, "Lolo! Don't forget your old Mama Lila, eh?" He hadn't deigned to turn around for a last good-bye. He walked with the same gait as his papa Gino, the same slight wagging of the head . . . Poor Lila! She'd dug out one of those horrid coats with a fox-fur collar, prewar shoes, a patent leather purse just for him. Her makeup was gaudy, she had on too much powder, her red lipstick ran over the edges of her lips.

The plane took off. Dejected, I followed it in the sky with my eyes for a long time until it became nothing but a small dot that was carrying Marcello far away from me. And Lila began smiling, and then laughing.

"It's as plain as day, Sybille! We've got to go to New York! Ha, ha, ha! I would never have expected this . . . after fifty years . . . I've got Henry's address over there. We mustn't wait any longer, eh? And I want you to be with me when I see Henry again . . ."

And from then on she hadn't mentioned Marcello again. She'd gotten over his departure in a very sudden fashion. Having regained her good spirits, she joked, rubbed her hands together, and thought of nothing but getting to America as quickly as possible. An imperious need for America, especially the urgent desire to be at Henry's side. She'd forgotten about the pain Marcello had caused us, about the tears shed, the words that had proven useless. We had each in turn threatened, implored, coddled him. I'd apologized to him a thousand times. A thousand times begged his forgiveness for my hundred lies. And Lila spoke of Life, its complications, the unforeseeable, as well as its dark side into which adults sometimes slip, get lost. She had explained the errors of youth, dragged around like bulky suitcases for years on end, from town to town, through the highs and lows of existence. Trunks that had long remained closed over the pain of lies, over slightly shady memories, the deprivation, the "I should have's," the omissions, and the sudden fears. Suitcases ripped open one day—by accident or out of lassitude—revealing obsolete secrets to stunned eyes, staggering revelations, shattered vials, chains, keys that could no longer open any door, testimony: compromising letters, outdated IOUs, and love letters. Marcello had frowned. She'd spoken to him of the tragedy of the war and postwar years, had explained the ration cards, the theater, and reckless love affairs. But, frayed as worn ropes, our words could not hold him back. "Guadeloupe" was the only word on his lips. He could see nothing but that horizon where his father reigned supreme, resuscitated by Marie La Jalousie, and the country that was waiting to be explored. Eyes filled with reproach, all that counted for him was the amount of time wasted and the number of things left unsaid.

At first, Lila refused to understand Marcello's anger. For her, his need for a father felt like a betrayal. "What use is a father," she would mumble, "since you have two mamas!" And then, little by little, the feeling had shifted. She ended up convincing herself that destiny was thumbing its nose at her. Repeated every day, "It's not to meet his father that he wants to go away, it's to hurt me! And it's true that it hurts me, Sybille! Oh, I suffer more than you do . . . Now that figures pretty well, you wouldn't believe how well that figures! But it's only fair! At seventy years of age, I would never have expected it . . ."

All the while, I felt ashamed of him and of myself. He would hold my gaze. He didn't want to remain docile anymore and put up with the ramblings Lila would launch into, never getting to the end of her sentences, mixing the past in with the present, daily events, and daydreams, the dead and the living in a bewildering fashion, drifting from one story and era to another, in a confusion that she seemed to master perfectly, but that always left us baffled.

She would harass him, "Why do you want to leave me again? I'm not afraid of anything anymore! Were you ever in need of anything? Tell me what you need . . . Tell me what your problem is!" She would implore him, "Don't leave your old mama, Marcello! This time I'll die if you go away . . . Your father's alive. So what? Why should we give a damn? He never had anything to do with you. It's not because Billy buried him too early that you should abandon us like this!"

She would repeat, "Don't go over there, Lolo! What difference does it make? You're black, I'm white! But I'm your mama all the same . . . And we couldn't care less about other people, isn't that right?"

After the reproaches, we stopped speaking to him, for nearly a month, so he'd be unhappy, tell us he still loved us, that the crisis had passed. We would fall silent when he came in. We ate in silence. And, feigning to be captivated by the images on the television, we no longer lifted our heads when he came home from his nights out with friends. I stopped greeting his new friends, West Indians from Paris or elsewhere, from some distant outskirts, that he brought to our house. He kept bad company, grass-smokers, bongo players with yellow, shifty eyes, half Rastafarians with multicolored knit hats, looking sly like thieves on the lookout, who jargonized in a Creole stuffed with English words. As for the girls, from the very start, I saddled them with all of the faults in the world, suspected them above all of turning him against us.

We already weren't talking to each other very much when we met Marie La Jalousie on the platform of the Raspail Metro Station. I couldn't handle him anymore. Marcello was seventeen years old, and there Marie was informing him that his father was still alive and that I had done nothing but lie to him from the beginning. It was exactly what he wanted to hear. He stopped speaking to me altogether, denigrated me, and stayed shut up in his room, sprawled on his bed, boots on, listening to music from the West Indies.

I asked him to forgive me; I told him the story about Gino and Marie. But we were never able to piece things back together. One evening in the month of March, he exclaimed, "I can see Guadeloupe! I can see my father! You think I'm here in this cage! But I'm over there. I'm as free as a bird. I'm flying with my father!" He was smiling and batting his wings. There was a provocative tone to his voice, and little bursts of hatred as well.

The next day, I went to buy his ticket at the travel agency on rue Victor-Hugo. He took off three days later. Up until the last minute, Lila was hoping that he would postpone the date of his departure and we would celebrate his birthday together, that he'd blow out his eighteen candles in Paris. He'd sworn to come back before September, in time to start his senior year.

America—after Marcello's departure, Lila endlessly chewed my ear off about it from March to June. She'd taken care of her passport without even knowing whether Henry would accept her coming. She sent off her letter in the beginning of April. A week later, she received a letter from America that she waved in front of my nose for nearly a quarter of an hour before reading it to me. Henry was waiting for her, wanted her to jump on the first plane for New York.

Henry hadn't remarried after the death of his wife, Lana. His children were successful. Michael was working for a large computer company on the West Coast. Rodgers was a car salesman; James-Lee cooked with his father at The Kreyol restaurant; and Sundra, a lawyer, had finally opened her office in an upper-class neighborhood in Harlem.

From March to June, Lila begged me to come with her. She would say, "I won't go without you, my Billy! I wouldn't have the strength! I can't go if you don't come . . . I'd hate to die without having seen Henry again . . . Take my blood pressure! My pulse is weak, Billy . . ."

When I would answer that I had to stay in Paris, in case Marcello came back before September, she'd shrug her shoulders and glare at me as if I were pretending to not understand.

"You'll get back together with your son! You have plenty of time for that! I have to go before it's too late. You don't realize how old I am, Billy! You don't see how worn out I am. You've got no pity. If I happen to bow out, you'll regret it. You have no idea how regrets can eat away at you! You're all I have left here, Billy!"

In the beginning of the month of June, Lila refused to eat. I didn't insist. Since Marcello had left, I wasn't eating real meals either. I nibbled a little at the hospital. When I got home, I'd settle down in front of the television and fret next to the telephone. Marcello rarely called. When I went to visit Lila, she'd spend the whole time unreeling her life. She'd always talk to me about her coming death, about America, and about Henry who was waiting for her. I resented her not being worried about Marcello, the fact that she'd wiped him out of her thoughts so quickly.

She'd begun to find it difficult to get around, to lift her feet, as if each step were a stair. She had conversations with the antennas and the electric wires on the building across the street, sang love songs to herself, and cried as she listened to Billie Holiday's voice in "God Bless the Child" and "When Your Lover Is Gone." I thought I knew her inside out. Her blood pressure was good for her age. Until I found her one evening unconscious, stretched out in the middle of the living room, I was convinced she was being theatrical. So then I prayed she wasn't dead, that she would have the time to go see her America. Implored God to grant her a bit more breath. And I trembled while the night doctor examined her looking doubtful. "She's seventy years old . . . You mustn't upset her anymore. Perhaps we should hospitalize her . . . " he said, scrawling the names of medicines on a prescription. "Are you a member of the family?" I promised to take Lila to consult her cardiologist and closed the door after a man with a stoop who seemed to be carrying all the illnesses diagnosed since nightfall on his shoulders.

"You didn't answer the doctor, Billy!" Lila yelled at me from her room.

"What are you talking about, Lila?"

"Well, are you a relative or not?"

Her face was distraught, eyelids heavy. I pictured her old worn out heart, ready to give way any second. So I sat down on the edge of her bed, and I whispered in her ear that I was her daughter and that we were going to fly to America soon.

Marcello called the next day. His voice betrayed a note of exaltation, which he was struggling to control. He spoke hurriedly. He had seen his father. Yes, Judes and Coraline were fantastic.

No! He wasn't smoking grass. Oh, he was so happy to be in Guadeloupe. He still hadn't gone to see his father's parents. He loved the country. It was cane harvesting season. There were carts on all the roads. He'd eaten cane! His father had taken him to go and taste some! For the first time in his life, he'd bit into a piece of sugar cane! He'd learned to suck and swallow the juice of a piece of sugar cane! Oh, he was truly enjoying Guadeloupe!!!

When I told him that Lila and I were soon going to leave for America, he had nothing to say, just, "Ah! That's good, how nice . . ."

8

On June 5, two days before leaving for the United States, I dozed off on Lila's couch and dreamt of Marcello, over there in Guadeloupe, following in Gino's footsteps. Judes and Coraline were also there. And so were Clothilde and my papa Robert, who died on a bed in a cabin in Basse-Terre. I saw myself as a child again, with Marie La Jalousie, Nitila's daughter, miming the famous lovers and singing those cruel songs from back in the old days . . .

Blood sausage hot
Blood sausage cold
The devil passed by that abode

Blood sausage hot
Blood sausage cold
Death passed by that abode . . .

I woke up with that refrain in my head. And the face of Marie La Jalousie filling my eyes. All of her faces at each stage in her life. Marie at the age of eight. Marie at twenty. Marie at thirty-nine . . .

On that particular morning, my old Lila was up, her mouth filled with words. So joyful to be leaving for America. She had to talk, stick words together . . . As if to fill up the gaps in the story of her life . . . As if to prepare me for meeting Henry, the illustrious ghost from her past. She had lined up the little vials, the crystal and porcelain bottles. She was finally gauging their contents and her mind seemed to be at rest. She was shaking them up, searching for the most evocative words to bring the old days, her lovers, and her war to a halt.

"Henry . . . oh yes, I can guarantee you, he helped me get over Hans. Can you believe it? A black man! I never would have believed I would find myself in bed with a black man. It's not the kind of thing you think about when you're twenty years old. You understand that, Billy! It just isn't customary. . . . Yet, at the time, I'd already known quite a few men. I can't even count how many, believe me . . .

"Henry . . . he was so dashing in his uniform. A beautiful wide smile under his khaki side cap . . .

"I'm not sure what got into me. I was sitting at the terrace of a café . . . It's funny, always meeting up with someone at a bistro, just like with Hans and so many others . . . At the Lucky-Charm, I believe it was. You won't have ever heard of it. It closed down two or three years after the war. The owner had been pretty mixed up in the black market. He'd been caught. He had a reputation for trafficking in wines from Spain and Portugal that old ladies would haul around in suitcases. And also large amounts of spirits that he would serve to his regular clients in tea cups. But he'd also hidden Jews, members of the Resistance, and Brits in his cellar among the bottles of wine, sacks of potatoes, and Bayonne hams. And that made people consider him to be a hero. I have no idea what became of him. His name was . . . I don't want to get it wrong . . . His name was . . . bah! It's not important anymore, Sybille. Who needs to know his name? After fifty years . . .

"You mustn't forget that the war turned everything upside down. We'd spent so many years living just one day at a time, we'd gotten used to it.

"To us, there was no longer any difference between right and wrong. We'd seen how the war had begun, the terrible way in which it had drawn out. What it had done to us . . . Maybe that's why I had so many lovers, Sybille. Maybe because of the war, I learned that you had to grab love when you had the chance. And not put on airs. And not let it slip through your fingers. Get the most out of your body . . . because that was all we had left . . . You get that, Sybille?

"Don't condemn me . . . There are too many judges on this earth . . . We needed it to numb ourselves, to stop feeling disgusted with the world that the war had smeared with mud and blood. To stop thinking about the armed men in the streets of Paris, the tanks, the armored vehicles, and the yellow stars . . . Persuade ourselves that life wasn't a nightmare, Billy. That we couldn't dream of a better one. And the scent of bodies making love, the fragrance of lovers filled the air . . . I believed I was eternal in the arms of my men, Sybille.

"Henry . . . that big strapping black man, amazed me. You know, throngs of girls went to the Lucky-Charm after work. It was the first time I'd set foot in there since Hans left in '43. Since the end of the war in fact . . . The girl that dragged me there was named Corinne. At the time, we were working together at Messaline Dedray. We sewed chic undergarments by hand, slips, panties, and brassieres for women who had the means of paying for the luxury of lace. We filled all types of jobs at Messaline, seamstresses, salesgirls, and maids too. We'd met each other at the theater. Corinne was incredibly talented. But in '52, she gave up her career when she fell under the spell of a funny old bird who became her husband. I can still picture her, cheeks flushed and lips pursed, when she announced she was quitting the theater out of love. "He asked me to choose, Lila . . . I'm happy, you can't begin to imagine. No, it's not a sacrifice, I'm madly in love with him. No, I won't regret it." Needless to say, twenty years later, I happened to run into her on the Boul'Mich. Worn out, that Corinne . . . Livid, broken. Divorced, five brats underfoot. And that old crow of hers, vanished along with the savings for a house in the suburbs they were going to buy. Flew the coop on the arm of some starry-eyed girl who wasn't half his age!

"Well, in the days of the Lucky-Charm, Corinne was fresh

and gorgeous. Henry appeared with three boys in uniform who were bawling out military songs. Four fellows. Two the color of black coffee, and the two others—one of which was Henry—were café au lait. They were on their fifth bar and were beginning to mix up English, French, and Creole as the alcohol clouded into their blood. The other girls were sitting on the laps of soldiers like so many decorative objects. People were necking like crazy. There were only us two, sitting alone at our table in front of our teacups waiting for love. They caught sight of us immediately. Henry was giving us the eye. I was a brunette that summer. Corinne, a redhead. A real one. With freckles, very fine, diaphanous skin. And gams as beautiful as a prima ballerina. We were nicknamed "The Inseparables." It lasted for the year I worked at Messaline. Then we lost touch with one another.

"We smiled at Henry. You know, that fatuous smile of girls who would give their bodies in no time at all but play stuck up to make believe they're virgins.

"I had hidden my affair with Hans from everyone. I didn't even want to remember it myself. But I was already suffocating from that secret. I'd never been out in public with him. We saw each other in my apartment. I might well have had my head shaved after the war if anyone had learned of it. Because, after all, he did have to climb all the way up here and pass people on the stairs and in the hallways . . .

"You have to try to imagine what it was like in those days . . . Summer of '44. You wouldn't believe how crazy the Liberation was . . . Crowds were dancing in the streets. Women were open-mouth kissing complete strangers. Our saviors in uniform! It didn't take Corinne and I long to fall into the arms of those black men! It was so exciting, you just can't imagine. We could feel their thighs harder than stone under our bottoms. There was no comparison with the white men we'd gone out with. At all, I can swear to that. They were, how should I put it . . . male, yes, but as if they'd come from another planet. And it made you tingle. Men cast in bronze . . . Yeah, that's it: bronze statues that had turned into flesh-and-bone men. Yeah, the bronze reflections had remained on their skin. And their smiles, Sybille. Like Gods, I'm not kidding you! Drunken Gods come down from heaven just for us two. Corinne and me.

"We sipped on whiskey. Almost three hours of having drinks paid for us. We didn't even notice when one black coffee and another café au lait disappeared. The four of us had been petting and necking to celebrate the victory, the end of the war, and the fire that was kindling in our bodies. The four of us sitting in front of our teacups filled to the brim with scotch . . .

"Corinne had inherited the tall black man. Jeffrey, if I recall, Jeffrey, who was a real American from America. Long fingers, blue nails. He had dancing in his blood, one helluvah swinger. He didn't just walk like everyone else, Jeffrey didn't. Had little clouds under his feet, bubbles or birds he was afraid of crushing. So, he bounced along, weightless, so lightly it lent us wings. Life didn't seem so oppressive by his side. When I saw Corinne twenty years later, we dug up old memories. Inevitably talked about our two black men . . . She, trampled underfoot by life that weighed down like a ton on her heart, and I, tormented by the phantoms of war, it cheered us up to talk about Jeffrey, the Swinger. We felt lighthearted for a time. We laughed, remembering our bodies of long ago, young and enticing, that yearned only for love.

"I had Henry all to myself. Café au lait black man. Amber-colored hair and pink lips. You can picture the type, Sybille. He talked endlessly about his mother, Jenny this, Jenny that. He gabbed about that Jenny of his all the way to the bedroom.

"By the way, the name of that actor came back to me last night: Harry Belafonte, it's his twin brother we're going to see in America. Yes ma'am, a spitting image of him! And I'm not exaggerating . . ."

Lila fell silent. But as she was drinking her black coffee in small sips, her mind had continued gathering up the memories of her love life with Henry.

The first evening, Henry had taken off his shoes, mumbling incomprehensible words from which the name Jenny, someone called Isidor, and the horseman Michael came drifting up to the surface. Then he had passed out on Lila's bed. She'd laid her head on his chest and gone to sleep in turn.

The next morning, Lila woke up first, with one hell of a headache, wondering why she'd brought a black man back to her apartment. She washed up in a hurry, powdered her cheeks, and smeared her lips with lipstick. Henry hadn't budged. She closed the door and hurried off to Messaline's.

Lila had spent the day listening to Corinne relate Jeffrey's exploits. While they fitted lace to panties, over the lunch break and late into the afternoon, Corinne bragged on endlessly about Jeffrey's amorous skills. According to her, her black coffee black man was a God parachuted into her bed. The kind of man that just doesn't exist on earth.

"A black man! Can you believe it, Lila? I would have liked to die in his arm it was so sublime. Three hundred times I saw myself way up close to the sun. He made me climb up to heaven, I swear he did, Lila!"

Henry was on leave. When Lila went home that evening, he was waiting in the living room, settled into an armchair, a glass of whisky in his hand, his long legs stretched out and crossed in front of him.

"I'm taking you to the Lucky-Charm, baby. Would you like that?"

She'd objected, "No, I'm feeling dizzy. I'm not going out. I'm going to go to bed." She'd slipped into her bed in the hope that he would get up and disappear from her life. But he followed her. Stretched out entirely dressed next to her. Began stroking her face. Then her hair. Her ears. The back of her neck. Kissed her gently on the temples. On her neck. On her breasts. He moved his lips slowly over her belly. Between her thighs. And Lila did not push him away. But rather, held his head between her hands. How long had they remained like that? She, petrified with pleasure, and he, patient, generous, attentive to her desire. How long before entering the state of ecstasy? When she decided for him to be inside of her, she loosened her fingers and their lips touched, tasted each other before finally being truly united.

How long did that kiss last? Lila hadn't the slightest idea. While he was growing rigid and weighing down upon her, bronze statue, he asked her permission to take off his pants. Without saying a word, Lila had undone the buckle of his khaki belt herself. Had undressed him. And then, skin against skin, their bodies had given themselves to one another. Black skin against white skin. Arms and legs mingled with sweat in the middle of that summer night in 1944. How long had he been lost within her? How long before he started talking to her of marriage?

When he'd stayed in Lila's apartment alone for that whole day, Henry had thought things over, striding back and forth across the bedroom and the living room. Head swimming with the perfume on a scarf draped over an armchair, he pictured himself back with his battalion, under enemy fire. They had to hold on for the night . . . December 1943. A campaign in Northern Italy. Everything was exploding all around them. And worst of all, there was screaming. Shrieks of fright. Begging . . . "My God! Oh my God, save us!" Voices twisted with pain. Grown suddenly deeper with the blood spurting into the throat. Mouths barely torn from their mothers' milk that hadn't had the chance to suck on other women's breasts. The women they dreamt of every night who were a consolation for being men-at-arms on this earth. The women who were all lips and bottoms, whom they penetrated in their dreams before sinking into black holes . . .

What a waste of green kids . . . White, black, red, yellow kids . . . Young boys, who, like him, had left a remote place in the Caribbean, in Northern Africa, in Asia, in the South Pacific, in America . . . to court death in Europe, sacrifice their lives in a conflict whose horror they had not fully assessed the extent of, whose causes they did not truly understand. A war in which they had volunteered with more than enough courage, and the sincere sentiment of belonging to the same France scattered about the world. A France that they loved and that they strove with all their heart to serve. So they obeyed, as well as they could, the orders of the Free French Division that had come to rally English and American troops that landed in Sicily in July of 1943.

White men who had drilled military discipline and the use of weapons into them. Leaders who thought of them as men. And who, as they drew nearer to the old continent, promised them every day the imminent end of the combat, war medals, and women galore, thanks to the glory that always follows in the footsteps of military men.

"What you going to do if you get out of this alive?" Asked a Martiniquais who was barely twenty. Isidor Deblavieux . . . Henry recalled him squatting behind his bush, rifle trembling in his hands. "What you got planned?"

"I'm getting married to the first girl who gives me her body for nothing. I swear to it in front of God," Henry had responded, before adding: "And you, what you dreaming of, Isidor?"

"I going back to Martinique as soon as the war is over and ask my mother forgiveness for calling her a whore because she had seven children with seven different fellars." Isidor wiped a tear from his cheek. "See, I didn't know nothing about life. When I left, I didn't even hug my mother, isn't that something, Henry? My mother Nini, I didn't even look at her when she started crying cause of me. Didn't even offer her a handkerchief. I kept on insulting her all the way out to the street. And then I got into a boat with some dissidents and went to the Dominican Republic where the recruitment officers of the Free French Forces were waiting for us."

"Yeah," Henry conceded, thinking of Jenny and of his father, George MacDowell. "You just never know what drives a woman to go to bed with a man . . ."

"Don't disrespect women, Henry! Don't never swear a woman is a slut. Your own mother and the others. Never bow so low as that . . . So, if I get out of this alive, swear to God, I going to beg Nini's forgiveness. I going back to tell her I sorry and admit that I ain't nothing but a poor fool. I going direct and kiss Nini's feet. And I going to thank her for having brought me into the world. For having carried me in her belly. And for having conceived me with two eyes that see straight, two valid legs, two arms, and . . ."

Isidor was hit in the chest. The machine gun fire wounded Henry in the arm in several places. Isidor didn't take long to die.

Fingers clenched over his rifle. Eyes open in order to conserve an image of life in which—perhaps—Nini had appeared in the midst of the bombing.

Henry was transferred to a military hospital. Was taken care of by women, voluntary nurses, trained in the field to bandage wounds and hold the hand of the dying. He hadn't experienced the Liberation of Paris. Neither had he paraded down the Champs Élysées, behind the victorious tanks of the Second Armored Division under the command of General Leclerc and the officers who had promised them a profusion of medals and women. He'd made his way up to Paris the week afterward.

And it's true; there were lots of women, offering their bodies to the liberators like those little flavored cakes that Jenny used to serve to Mrs. MacDowell's guests at tea time. They didn't pay any attention to color. They stuck out their mouths to the first man who came along. Their red lips like *cerises*-cherries pasted on the bottom of their faces. Their cheeks flushed with the August heat. Their sapphire and emerald eyes fluttering under the black accent of their brows. Their hair in little curls and crinkles. Their white skin. So pale, my friend . . . And the impudent wind that made sure to lift their skirts and reveal other appealing attributes. Shapely legs, rosy thighs, garters, and white and baby blue lace. Women had invaded the streets, the sidewalks, the balconies, the windows of the buildings, waving the flag of peace. Paris was a woman in Henry's heart. Paris in red, white, blue, and pink . . . emblems of freedom.

That's what the capital city of France seemed like to Henry in the days following the Liberation. A land of shared happiness in which the victors were triumphing. A land of free love. A land of paradise that he was proud to have fought for, even though he wasn't able to forget the brothers in arms who'd been torn to bits, who would soon be no more than names at the bottom of war memorials.

Lila was the first girl to give her body to him for nothing. God! A Parisian! A little brunette with the name of a flower. As Isidor would have put it, now that's a stroke of luck for you! A little white doll with big blue eyes, like his father, George MacDowell.

• • •

"That rotten George MacDowell! What's he want now?

"Oh that lousy, vile George MacDowell, when you going to stop catering to his whims, Mummy? How much longer you going to treat him like a poor bloke?"

Jenny remained silent.

"Oh, Mum! Let him go on ringing his bell! Let him keep on ringing it till he comes over here so I can spit the truth in his face and call him daddy till it burns his heart and ears. I wish he'd die! And you won't never catch me crying over his grave!

"He a vile man!"

Jenny didn't bat an eyelash. She continued turning the spoon in her cast iron pot, continued kneading her dough, continued spooning finely cut vegetables around the leg of lamb. She showed not the slightest trace of emotion, convinced that the rancor gnawing at Henry would blow over with time.

She'd waited until he was fifteen to admit to him that George MacDowell was his father, and not Michael, at whose grave he had knelt for so many years. Between his mother and Peggy Douglas, whom he called Auntie Peggy, he had prayed every day for the soul of Michael, who had died a tragic death at the age of twenty. People claimed he was an exceptional horseman. A fantastic rider according to the blacks on the plantation with whom the child shared snatches of stories and silences that plunged him into the mists of a confused past that he fed with the fruit of his imagination. Tales and legends of Michael and Columbus, James Henry MacDowell's horse, upon which he had fled. Story of engagement, of drinking, and regalement. Parables of dead birds found in his pockets. Mysterious saga that fired Henry's mind, grew ever larger in his dreams.

It was only after Peggy's death that Jenny had been able to free herself of the secret she'd been hiding inside since Henry's birth. A deleterious secret, destroying her flesh like a dead child in her entrails. A secret that might possibly lead Henry down the same paths of despair that Michael had journeyed. Poor Michael . . .

Peggy Douglas had left this world in her sleep. Called to her bedside in the morning, the doctor had diagnosed a heart attack. Jenny informed George a little before breakfast. Every morning at eight o'clock sharp the MacDowell family would gather. George's aging parents—James Henry, suffering from gout, and Elizabeth, who had contracted Parkinson's; his wife Kathleen—endlessly agitated with febrile gaiety, excessively exuberant and cheerful, like the birds in her aviary that flew around in circles in their jail; and lastly his children—Donald, Sherryl and Richard—who would have nothing but luxury and who spurned, as did their mother, the black servants in a deeply disdainful manner.

"Peggy Douglas is no longer with us, Master George . . . And today I am going to inform Henry that you are his papa," Jenny had declared.

George had succeeded his father as head of the factories, the import-export offices, and mills in England that he managed with an iron hand along with the fields of sugar cane on the immense property of Hamilton's Gardens. He spent one-fourth of his time overseas. And the events shaking Europe in that year of 1938 directly affected his interests, worried him more than the domestic affairs that he left in Jenny's hands. Though she continued to share half of his nights, he no longer felt so taken with her. At thirty-four years of age, George was so obsessed with the dread of losing a single penny, he was now an irascible man, prisoner to that other side of himself that it was his duty to embody—in the eyes of the whites on the island, in those of his family, and in those (still a bit moist) of Jenny Pierce who'd conceived their child on the night of December 18 in 1923. It was during that same night that he had felt the first pains deep in his stomach. Since then, they had never left him in peace. He had married Kathleen, and his ulcer at the same time, in Saint Gregory's chapel. Had watched his illegitimate son grow up from a distance while swallowing stomach powders. And, gritting his teeth, dealt with all of his affairs.

When Jenny informed him of Peggy's death, George felt a steely spike piercing his entrails. He immediately saw himself as a child again, running around Peggy whom he smothered with kisses . . . In his Little George body, infatuated with Suzan, Peggy's daughter, with whom he played at making the motions of love, exchanged oaths and bamboo rings . . . Little George standing petrified before the tall trees of Hamilton's Gardens, their immense branches from which black men had hung in the old days. Little George crying and hiccupping, head buried in Peggy's corsage, begging her to tell him stories about Mister Rabbit, Friend Elephant, and Sir Tiger . . . so he could forget the faces of Nanny and Percy, the heroic lovers that were the pride of the black people on the plantation . . . stop hearing the ghostly cries and clamors of the slaves once chained there, cries that still filled the hidden corners, the silences of Hamilton's Gardens.

Peggy would dry his tears and wipe his nose with her vast white apron. "Poor little Master George! Don't cry, child!" she would exclaim mockingly, before serving him some lime drink. Then she would console him with the tales in which animals had human adventures. That's when Peggy's eyes became two islands of light that held all of George's fears at bay as she went on.

Dazed by the wave of memories, George stood there for a moment contemplating Jenny, overwhelmed with the desire to bury his head between her breasts and sob as he used to when he was the child who was allowed to feel grief and fear.

For a moment he asked himself if Peggy Douglas had at times coddled his son Henry, dried his tears with the same kindness. But he maintained the same reserve he always observed in broad daylight. Simply delegate his power: "I'll see you this evening . . . You'll make all the necessary arrangements, Jenny! And let me know what time the funeral will be . . ." Then he had gone back to his people. Had not even considered saying a prayer for Peggy before they dug into the baskets of muffins and puckered out their pink lips toward the cups of boiling tea. He spoke of the upheavals in Europe with his father and the man called Hitler who'd had the gall to annex Austria and was preparing to invade Czechoslovakia.

"Who will stop him?" asked George.

"The water, George! The water!" cried James Henry MacDowell, raising his cup. "The Channel will bar his passage . . . He won't set foot in England, rest assured of that . . . "

"And France?"

"What about France? The Old World begot this little monster, George . . . The Old Continent bursting with pretentiousness . . ."

"Hitler will demand France as well . . . The Munich Conference proved how weak the Allies are."

While teaspoons tinkled in the fine porcelain cups and the cakes, slices of bread with orange marmalade, and cookies disappeared from the table, the two men continued talking about Europe, speculating about the probable war and ways of making a profit from it. Kathleen took advantage of a moment of silence to inform the elderly Mrs. MacDowell that the Queen had by that time baptized the ocean liner *Queen Elizabeth*.

"Prospective cruises to look forward to, isn't that so? Why don't we go away this summer, George? You aren't unaware of my curiosity with regards to Egypt. You already promised me last year, didn't you? I've been wanting to sail up the Nile for so long . . . Photograph the pyramids . . ."

"But, Kathleen!" cut in George dryly. "We'll soon be at war, and all you can think about are your little pleasure trips!"

Kathleen had been dying to fulfill that dream since Richard, her last child, had been born. George had always come up with a thousand pretexts to thwart her plans to get away. She hadn't left the Caribbean for nearly eight years now, making do with short escapades to her relatives and friends scattered around from the Bahamas to Tobago.

Kathleen had brought back a sudden passion for birds from a stay in Jamaica with her cousin, Jessica Eddington, who owned an aviary that resembled a gazebo set up in the middle of the garden. An aging beauty, Jessica had always found fault with the suitors who came calling. She therefore lived alone on California Dream, the property of her deceased parents. Lawyers, notaries, and bankers made certain her fortune multiplied. Numerous black people saw to the upkeep of her lands. Black women cleaned her house from cellar to attic, washed her clothes, prepared her meals, fixed her hair, and guarded her sleep. Jessica's principal activity was going out to admire the impeccable lawns of California Dream, and then going to throw seeds to the birds in her aviary. As the years went by, when her first wrinkles and bitter feelings appeared, she had stopped making the rounds of the salons in Jamaica where she suspected mockery behind every face, believing that the married women laughed behind her back, giggled, snickered, and jabbered inanely about her idle life. To that futile prattle, Jessica preferred the chirping of her dear little creatures who gave meaning to her gilded retreat.

Upon returning to Hamilton's Gardens, Kathleen had immediately given the order for a gazebo identical to Jessica's to be made and filled with birds of all species. From it, she drew a comical sense of glory, an artificial industriousness, and outrageous enthusiasm. A mandatory detour for MacDowell visitors—forced to go into raptures over it until their smiles turned to grimaces—Kathleen's aviary was Henry's way of wreaking revenge when, at fifteen years of age, his mother revealed to him the name of his true father: George MacDowell . . .

Up until the day of Peggy's last journey, Henry had always thought of George MacDowell as an austere, distant, curt, always shifty-eyed man. The master of Hamilton's Gardens, with whom he hadn't exchanged more than ten sentences since he'd been living by his mother's side in a little house located not far from the kitchens. They would pass one another at times. George at the wheel of his automobile, a Citroën 7 that he'd bought in France, or else astride Saturn, his chestnut horse; Henry on the way to the Baptist school where Rose, Peggy's daughter, was the schoolteacher. They avoided one another intuitively.

At a very young age, Henry had decided of his own accord to fill the place at Jenny's side that had been left vacant by Michael, his supposed father. And he chided his mother for slaving for the MacDowells, for working harder than necessary, for wearing herself out for those white people who looked down on their black servants. Often, he would rebel against Jenny's zealousness, seeing her scurrying around to better serve George, her lord and master, to whom she vowed a sort of mystical adoration akin to that of some dutiful slave. Henry didn't understand what that devotion was based on, and even less the motivation behind it. He hated her when she bemoaned the poor health of the master of Hamilton's Gardens, mortified herself for him. It's true that Henry never saw a sign of recognition from George. The man only let his cold mask down during the hours of intimacy he spent with Jenny. At those times, he turned back into the young man of twenty who had scratched at Jenny's door like a dog one evening . . . The young man that he sometimes saw in Henry's tall silhouette, in the way he walked, and tilted his head to one side.

"Oh, he a vile man!" he would grumble to Jenny when they were alone in the kitchens shelling the peas for dinner. "I happy knowing his stomach tortures him. There a bunch of black men in his belly, Mum! They all in there, the black men of centuries of slavery, the ones who died under the whip of the old masters of Hamilton's Gardens. And they gnawing and knocking around. It's only fair in the end, ain't that right?"

After Peggy's funeral, Jenny had held him back by the sleeve as he began to head over toward Michael's grave. She murmured, "We can't be dawdling, Henry! I got things to tell you . . ."

Henry listened to her, not understanding.

And while they were heading homeward, she gathered the words with which to confess her secret to him, convinced that the truth would chase from Henry's mind the evil spirit that prevented him from judging George at his true worth . . . A good, loving, incomparably gentle man. A man filled with a thousand fears who loved black people more than whites. The man who had been her very own for the last sixteen years.

"So, now Peggy is gone, Henry!"

"Yes, Mum!"

"Now you need to stop thinking about Michael so much."

"And why is that, Mum?" he replied, glaring at her the same way as George MacDowell did. "Why is it I should stop thinking about my father now that Auntie Peggy's left us?"

Jenny smiled. At thirty-two, she was still a beautiful woman. And Henry put her on a pedestal, proud that she didn't allow other black men from Hamilton's Gardens to court her, that she remained entirely loyal to Michael's memory.

"I got to tell you what Miss Peggy always refused to let you know . . . It's that Michael wasn't your father, Henry . . . Your father is Master George . . ."

Henry took the news like a bullet straight to the chest. His body was knocked backward, and he tore himself from Jenny's hands, which were trying to hold him back. Suzan and Rose, Peggy's two daughters, as well as the Baptist friends who were coming back from the cemetery with them, believed he was running away to hide his grief. And no one thought any more about it.

Six years later, leaning on his elbows gazing out of Lila's window, finding himself at the end of the war in which he had lost so many friends, Henry was remembering his flight through the woods. He'd run off as swiftly as the horse Columbus upon whose back poor Michael had leapt to go in search of his death. He'd galloped away so that the horror that was so close on his heels wouldn't catch up with him. Truth that Jenny was trying to make him swallow with placid revelations, liberated as she was from her chains after the death of Auntie Peggy. Abomination always glimpsed in the mirrors reflecting the hazy tales and legends from which the figure of his father rose heroically. Poor, sordid reality setting its traps in order to destroy Michael's image, conceived with such pugnacity during all those years of deception.

Jenny thought he'd disappeared forever, just as poor Michael had. But he came home in time to help her prepare the dishes for the MacDowells.

"So it's really him, Mum?" he murmured without looking at her, chopping the onions and the bell peppers for the preserves that were to accompany the leg of lamb. "It's George MacDowell?"

Jenny nodded her head.

"And why didn't you ever tell me, Mum?"

"Well, because of Miss Peggy . . ."

"And just what did Auntie Peggy have to do with it?"

"She didn't want you to know. She didn't want to admit you were illegitimate. Peggy was always saying; 'White folk with white folk. Black folk with black folk, and the world will keep on turning round.' She swore it wasn't natural for people of different colors and conditions to love each other. And it was better for you to have a dead father rather than a white one."

"And he obeyed Peggy's orders too?"

"He couldn't go against his past . . ."

Henry laughed bitterly. "Ha! Ha! Ha! The master of Hamilton's Gardens! Not free to recognize his own son. Not free to say to Sir James Henry, 'Oh, Dad! I got a son who sleeps over there with the kitchen maid. He ought to come eat his meals at our table . . .'"

Overwhelmed with grief, he'd wept. Brokenhearted tears of rage.

At the age of eighteen, Henry had torn himself away from Michael's ghost, turned his back on his island, on Jenny, and on that unacceptable white father. He'd gone to Guadeloupe, to the town of Sainte-Rose, where Hypolite Grosval had taught him the ironworking trade and the French language. At twenty-two, he chose to be a dissident and join General de Gaulle.

And then he'd arrived in Paris where that girl Lila had given him her body for nothing, and he'd promised himself he would ask her to marry him.

9

"Marriage!" Lila had been startled at first, then burst out laughing.

"Think it over for a couple of days, okay? You can give me your answer later," Henry said stroking her dark curls with the tips of his fingers.

"A couple of days! That's just not the way it's done! We don't take getting engaged lightly over here . . ."

He fell silent for a moment before going back to relating the story of George MacDowell whom he had once thought of as a weak, despicable being.

"My mother devoted her life to him. She would always go running as soon as the bell rang, running to take him his stomach powders, anticipate his slightest desires."

It was the end of September 1944. Whenever Henry was on leave, he would hurry over to see Lila, who opened her bed to him and offered her body for him to taste and penetrate. She couldn't come to a decision over the marriage question. Despite Henry being under the illusion that the deplorable problems between blacks and whites were a thing of the past, Lila couldn't picture herself with a black man. A whole lifetime! He believed people thought of him as a man. Simply a man . . . He had been one of France's saviors, and, in his mind, that victory erased all prejudice against blacks.

• • •

When Jenny revealed the identity of his father, Henry had taken off through the woods like a mad dog till he reached the gardens of the domain, screaming out Michael's name so he would come back from amongst the dead and cut down George MacDowell who'd stolen Jenny's heart, begging Michael to come down and wreak revenge on the white world of Hamilton's Gardens. The only thing those people knew how to do was bark out orders, keep others in servitude, and think exclusively of their personal well-being. "Poor Michael! Poor Michael!" He pictured Auntie Peggy. Once again heard the two words she had whispered in his ear so often. "Poor Michael! Poor Michael! Rode off on Columbus when he was engaged to your mama . . . The day after the engagement party, he mounted Sir James Henry MacDowell's horse. And then disappeared. We don't know why . . . No one ever came up with an explanation . . . But he loved you before you were born. He used to say, 'I waiting for my son as ardently as I am for the Messiah. And Jenny and I going to have other children, going to found a fine family . . .' His life seemed to be all cut out for him . . . And then, no one understood what went wrong. Maybe too much brandy. Some folk say it was overwhelming joy that struck him down. But the most mysterious thing about it was the little dead bird found in the pocket of his jacket. A poor creature destined to share the same fate. And Michael died just as he was starting to flap his wings and dream of flying for the rest of his life, alighting on different horizons. Jealousy got something to do with it, that's for sure," Auntie Peggy moaned. "If not, how you explain a young man going out searching for death till he finds it? Somewhere there's a culprit who must surely be paying dearly for having sent death out onto Michael's path. The Good Lord knows his name! And your mama who was carrying you in her belly, grieving. So much pain at having lost her sweet love . . ."

"And what happened to the dead bird he had in his pocket, Auntie Peggy?" asked Henry.

"Well, we put it in the coffin with Michael. We didn't know what to do with it. So we thought if it was a wicked thing, it couldn't do no more harm to anyone. And if it was a favorable sign, then its place was by Michael's side. I remember an old woman began telling the woeful tale that had caused the black slaves at Hamilton's Gardens to rebel. Long ago, the old Master MacDowell tried to separate a man and a woman who were in love. Nanny and Percy . . . sell the man to one of his distant relatives on the other end of the island and keep the woman for pleasure in his bed. First, they tried to flee, follow the paths to freedom leading away from Hamilton's Gardens. But they'd failed, been caught by the dogs that, back in those days, were ferocious guards trained to scent out a black man miles away. They killed themselves in despair. She took poison, and he hung himself. Strung himself up to a tree that's still standing. The old woman claimed that their love had refused to die with them and had metamorphosed into a bird. A bird that wasn't from our lands. That not a soul had ever seen spread its wings around our parts. A bird whose colors we sometimes admired in the last glimmers of daylight, when the sun looked like a glowing gourd floating for an instant out on the sea. But some swore it was the soul of the child that had been nestling in Nanny's belly that had broken loose before she let out her last breath. A soul without a body, roaming the earth that had been swallowed by a bird gulping down flies on a branch. An innocent bird that, enriched with that human soul, had been transformed into a rare species. Crossing themselves ostensibly, still others claimed that the Lord had come down to earth to resolve the problem. For He alone was able to decide the hour of death. He could not tolerate that ordinary beings dare take themselves for gods. Lickety-split, He looked around for a body to place that soul in. But the sun was going down. The Good Lord wasn't seeing clear no more. And so He entrusted it to a little bird who had built its nest in a traveler's tree, bidding it to give it back as soon as a body was available. Keeping its promise, the bird was very patient. But, the call of duty having led Him off to other places, the affair slipped the Good Lord's mind. That's how the bird inherited the human soul that proved to be quite cumbersome, for it gave rise to feelings and emotions, memories, and desires. Yearnings for affection, heartbroken adoration, grief-stricken affliction . . . The little bird tried to rid himself of it. As soon as the Good Lord had his back turned, he would chirp his head off but couldn't shake the soul loose. It stuck there, come rain or come snow. So the bird waited for death, to be free of that life of torment. Though it grew older, like any ordinary bird, the lost soul never returned to the human race; it chose a different bird that would carry the soul of Nanny's child from island to island. Generations of birds have borne that terribly heavy soul aloft . . ."

Depending upon his mood, Henry had a penchant for one or the other version. But most of the time, those tales got muddled up in his heart, always leading him to dream up enchanted worlds beyond the tangible worlds he encountered. And when he heard cheeping in one of the trees in Hamilton's Gardens, he would immediately imagine it was the lost soul come back to the scene of the tragedy so that an inanimate body would harbor it at last. On angry days, Henry would call to the rare bird, whistle until his throat and lips burned. At times like that, he dreamt of bringing together all the feathered creatures in the sky. Legions of them to destroy Hamilton's Gardens, its varnished paneling, its embroidered tablecloths, its carpets made in India, and those loathsome portraits in which the ancestors of George MacDowell smiled arrogantly, those very same people were alive when Nanny and Percy had killed themselves, when the Good Lord had the power to take love in his hand like a ball, a seed, or a sweet pepper and stuff the body of a sparrow with it. The vengeful birds born of his imagination would swoop down on the immense paintings, peck out the eyes, devour the noses, and pierce the bluish lips of the ancestors. Tear out their hair, their beards, and their mustaches, one hair after the other, to build nests by the thousands in the gardens of Hamilton. They would tear their ruffled shirts, their silk and satin dresses, their striped jackets and ties to shreds, and tie them to the kites of the little black boys of Saint John . . .

It was because of the legends Auntie Peggy related to explain the small dead bird found in Michael's pocket that Henry's rage led him to Mrs. Kathleen MacDowell's aviary. So many species collected throughout the Caribbean to chatter, jabber, titter before the island's white people. Such beautiful plumage behind the wire cage, flitting from one perch to the next, melancholy and indifferent. And singing the story of Nanny and Percy, as well as that of Jenny and Michael . . .

Henry stood there for a long time, observing the birds, torn between the hope of hearing one of them admit that hidden snugly under its feathers was a human soul, bestowed unto it by God, and the imperious urge to set them free to do justice to Nanny and Percy, to Jenny and Michael, and to the enslaved black men who'd never had the right to be more than mere possessions in the hands of the whites at Hamilton's Gardens.

The key to the aviary was kept in a small case inlaid with pearls that Mrs. Kathleen always carried with her. A tiny, finely gilt metal key, with flowers set into its basket-shaped bow. The door was of cast iron wrought into interlaced rosettes, identical to those that decorated the headboard of her mahogany bed covered with a mosquito net embroidered with the same motifs. Henry made his way around the gazebo. Night was setting in slowly, and most of the birds were dozing in the dead branches of a large-sized *Ficus elastica* that Kathleen had ordered be planted in the aviary. The shrub had gradually lost its leaves one by one. Since then, it looked like an old scarecrow upon which the sparrows hung their sorrow. Three nests, made of bits of string, twigs, strands of wool, and colorful cloth, sat sleepily in its branches.

First Henry tried to force open a small wooden shutter that was once used for putting earthenware dishes of water inside. Several birds having taken the opportunity to escape during those operations, Kathleen had condemned it. Then rust had welded the hinges tight. The shutter refused to open. Henry wept with rage. Powerless, he lit into the aviary, punching and kicking at it, cursing the generations of MacDowells . . . "My father, George MacDowell!" he repeated to himself in disgust. "George MacDowell! George MacDowell!" Suddenly, from the center of the gazebo arose a voice exactly like Auntie Peggy's. "Poor Michael! Poor Michael!" it chanted.

Then he pictured Peggy resuscitated, glassy-eyed in her coffin . . . "Poor Michael! . . . Poor Henry! They traded in your hero for George MacDowell, whom you never liked . . . Poor Henry! You going to find the strength to save them, and then it's up to you to win your freedom; if not, the MacDowells going to lock you up. Just as they done with your poor mama Jenny . . . She didn't deign to listen to me. Yet I warned her, 'White folk with white folk! Black folk with black folk! And the world will keep on turning round right nice and for a good long time to come . . .' And look what happened to that poor Michael . . ."

Roused by Peggy's wrath, Henry leapt up and managed to grab hold of the grating that girdled the cage under its wood shingle roof. The birds were already flitting about, letting out frightened squawks, seeking refuge in the upper branches of the ficus. One shingle, then two, then three tumbled to the ground. "Vile man! I hate him!" he growled to silence Peggy who was singing Michael's misfortune to the tune of a gospel song: "Vile man! Lousy, vile man! Vile! Vile! Vile!" When he began to twist the grating to set the birds free, his heart began to beat to the rhythm of music that seemed to be rising from beyond the grave.

The light was waning over Hamilton's Gardens. The full moon night slowly filled with the cries and stridulations of nocturnal insects. Allied beasts, free and powerful, "acolytes of Satan's sacristans," assured Peggy and then added, "You can't stay out late in the gardens of Hamilton, Henry! There are beasts . . . and also spirits from the past prowling round. They won't never go away. Don't go getting in their way, Henry! At night, faces ain't nothing but masks. Animals, men. And men, demons. You might think you chatting with one of our folk, but in truth you'd be confiding your soul to Lucifer. There's all kinds of creatures hanging round. Don't never let them sneak up on you, Henry! Even the masters of Hamilton's Gardens don't dare go out. They familiar with the traps . . . They know all too well what went on in the dark centuries when the black man was nothing but a stick of furniture. And there's the vermin you can't see, that you only hear in the darkness, the ones that gabble in tongues you can't understand. Now that kind are helpers for the others . . . Sometimes they manage to hold back the night, like a blanket over the day so that one last tragedy can be performed. So don't go and get yourself trapped . . ."

As he ripped off the grating, Henry could feel the blood throbbing in his temples, which gave him an incomparable feeling of jubilation. Peggy's song was slowly fading away. He wasn't afraid any more. He was the master of that night, master of Hamilton's Gardens, ready to face all the devils that could possibly appear.

It wasn't until morning that the birds took flight, in single file, relegating the aviary to the lone ficus and to Kathleen's despair, who cried over her little escapees for a long time.

"She never knew it was my work, Lila. Never suspected the cook's son . . ."

"And why are you telling me about that, Henry. What do I care about these damned bird stories?"

"Are you kidding, baby? You don't get it or what? It's that I'm finished with all that nonsense! I don't have anything against white people anymore. I don't have a grudge against George MacDowell anymore. And the two of us are going to get married, eh? I don't believe in Peggy's sayings anymore, 'White folk with white folk! Black folk with black folk, and the world will keep on turning round!' I've been through the war. I sat trembling beside our poor boys as they died, just like that, snap! The time it took me to turn around, they were dead. So, the two of us are going to get married because those days are over with, isn't that right, Lila? And I'm going to let you in on a secret . . . You are the first girl who gave me her body for nothing since I arrived in France. You're everything I ever wanted in life, Lila! I've forgiven my father, poor George MacDowell. Jenny did what she did out of love. I understood that too late. And I really think he loved her too. And it made him sick not to live his life with her out in the open and to have to put up with that Kathleen whom his mother had chosen for him. I'm going to explain something else to you too. You know, when they found the aviary empty of its little birds, well, George MacDowell laughed. He laughed, I swear to God . . . Not with his mouth, but with his eyes . . . He was happy. Happy to not have that jail sitting there in the middle of his garden. He laughed with his eyes . . . And I even think we looked at each other for the first time since we'd been passing one another without ever . . ."

"Sybille, I swear . . . Henry thought it was a miracle he hadn't been killed. He'd been through such a rough time, he couldn't bear the hate in his heart anymore. He'd been around too many cadavers, seen too much flesh blown apart, too many mutilated bodies. He told me that after the incident with the aviary, he didn't stay much longer at Hamilton's Gardens. He lost interest in school. And little by little, he stopped cursing George, because Jenny's eyes would brim with tears. But he wasn't able to accept the idea of having been dragged onto that raft of lies that his mother and Auntie Peggy had been navigating together for such a long time, of having knelt down for so many years between the two of them before Michael's grave, in plain sight of the black folk at Hamilton's Gardens who knew the truth and didn't intervene, except with those silences they dug into the middle of their tales. He hated himself for having been so credulous, for having learned too late about the tragic story of poor Michael, who hung himself from one of Hamilton's Gardens' tall trees—Mrs. MacDowell's pride and joy—that had already served as a gallows for some poor guy named Percy.

"That's why he ran away to Guadeloupe in 1942, Billy. He promised Jenny he was leaving to learn to be a horse groom, in order to further cultivate the memory of the phantom horseman who had enchanted his childhood. But as you know, life will start tracing other paths under our feet. We believe that our heart is a trustworthy compass pointing faithfully northward. We decide to be this, and we end up being that . . . Instead of becoming a hostler, Henry began an apprenticeship with an iron worker. He would sometimes see horses come through Hypolite Grosval's workshop, as he also served as a blacksmith. Henry would take the docile steeds of the foremen over to a field of cane perched up around Conodor, in Sainte Rose. He hardly thought of Michael anymore . . . Then at the liberation, while he could have chosen some nice woman who would have immediately accepted his marriage proposal, he ran into me, Lila . . .

"I wasn't the one who should have crossed his path. When he'd finished describing his life in Saint John to me, he insisted I talk to him about my childhood and my parents. I didn't have much to say, except that I'd left my village, Maillet, in Sarthe, and come to Paris at eighteen with a Parisian family who spent their vacations at the residence of Monsieur de la Garoncière, the local aristocrat. I told everyone I was going to be their maidservant in Paris. In truth, I already dreamt of being an actress. I couldn't picture myself as a farmer's wife, milking cows, making rillettes for my man, drinking cider, and having a baby every year, like my sisters, who thought marriage would make them into women and found themselves at twenty-five with sagging breasts and thick waists. A thousand dreams were crowding in my mind. At home I was nicknamed The Marquise. When I was little, I played with Monsieur de la Garoncière's children. I copied their mannerisms, and I had developed expensive tastes from being in their company.

"Henry saw the reflection of his own story in mine. Both of us had grown up in the shadow of rich people. We'd left that environment to try our luck elsewhere. And we met in Paris. Henry was always looking for magic everywhere. He kept repeating, 'We don't always understand what drives us. And then at some point, everything suddenly becomes clear! The two of us, we're forever, Lila!'"

10

The plane had just taken off. It was Lila's maiden flight, but she didn't show any signs of apprehension.

"At last, we're on our way! America, here we come, my little Billy!"

We exchanged a smile. Our hands met. Lila was pretty . . . I had fixed her hair and put on her makeup myself that morning. I'd picked out her clothes. And she'd let herself be fussed over like a young girl going to her first dance with her boyfriend. In the tone of her voice and her facial expressions, the young woman she had once been was struggling to erase the years.

"Fifty years, Lord! It doesn't add up to much, Billy! I can picture it as if it were yesterday . . . Henry, my café au lait black man! My heart is all aflutter. You'll understand when you're my age! If I try, I can even feel the weight of his body on mine. My man of bronze. And his long, velvet fingers. I can hear his voice as if it were yesterday, 'When are we going to get married, Lila? When will you give me your hand? When will we go before the mayor? You're my little flower that I picked in Paris. To Paris, forever . . .'"

While Lila pored over her memories, I was thinking of Gino, Marcello's father. Gino, mouth crawling with lies and head stuffed with women's names. Lila's love life far outdid mine. So I listened to her, like anyone who enjoys a good love story. Out of envy and curiosity. The desire to once again live through that constant upheaval, all the way to the breaking point. The waiting, the melancholy, the 'I love you's', the tears, the theatrics . . . The need to palpitate and shudder . . . Burn your body, hard! The thirst for caresses and kisses. Violent embraces. Secret passions . . .

"I didn't deserve him, Billy. I didn't accept his proposal. I don't really know why. Maybe because after a while, we French women sobered up. Blacks turned back into blacks in the eyes of white people. And the saga of the saviors was stowed away and forgotten. We continued eating out and hanging around in bars. But when Henry wasn't wearing a uniform, we were treated to some unpleasant remarks concerning white women who paraded around with black men. I felt uncomfortable. I refused to let him hold my arm or kiss me in the street. And he didn't understand a thing. He insisted, 'They're like Auntie Peggy, those people! They still believe that the world will keep turning round as long as blacks and whites don't mix . . .'

"I didn't remain in the service of the Parisians for long. I dug up a job as a waitress in a club, around Montparnasse. I became a hostess in a week. I earned a little extra money filling in as a naked dancer . . . but it was no El Dorado! Too far a cry from the world of theater . . . I sold perfume in the market places. In the beginning of the war, I was a maid at the Hotel Sextus, rue Alfred-Chicot. I already told you about that, Sybille. You must think I'm rambling . . . But I want you to know I was no better than those girls who worked by day and dreamt all night long of rivaling Morgan, Mistinguett, or Garbo. I said a few lines on stage, but I was only a double and never got any applause, or had any fans. All in all, I went to three drama classes. I was just a theater usher at The Rex for two months. At the end of the war, I found that job as a seamstress at Messaline Dedray.

"Henry was always a dreamer. See Sybille, there's just no room on this earth for people who say 'forever'. They waste their time scanning the sky for the age-old dreams of eternity. They talk to the birds and are convinced that people are flowers. He called me his little flower from France, his bouquet of lilacs. I'm not kidding, the pigeons in Paris were attracted to him. When we went to sit at the terrace of the Lucky-Charm, they flocked over by the score to rub up against his pant legs. And the same was true of the sparrows. It always impressed me. . . . When you see that, you're tempted to believe, just for a second, that 'forever' has meaning . . . Wings spring from your back. You think you're a bird or a flower. But then other people's looks catch hold of you and you find yourself sitting flat on the ground.

"Henry could send me straight to heaven . . . Just when I was about to tell him, 'Let's call it quits, Henry! I don't want us to see each other anymore . . . Go on back to your island to be with your birds and your mama Jenny. Get out of my life, far away! Go far away from Paris! Go on back to the place where there are stories of love that never dies! This is Paris! Nothing lasts here! Today it's you; tomorrow it'll be over . . . Here people don't talk to birds! Here 'forever' doesn't exist! Today you're a liberator of France, you get decorated like a Christmas tree, and tomorrow you're nothing but a darkie, a coon who's eating French people's bread. You're not wanted here, Henry . . .'

"He didn't even let me begin. He objected, 'Oh, I'm in no hurry, Little Flower! I can wait for you till the day I die.'

"Sybille, I got pregnant for Henry! You know, I tried to get rid of the kid. Nice and neat! Yeah, right! He was beside himself, happy as a lark, ready to marry me. He had been demobilized since December and had gotten hired on in a restaurant, avenue du Maine. He dreamt of the two of us walking in step behind a baby carriage. I didn't want to have anything to do with all that. No kid. No marriage . . ."

"Sybille, the abortionist stuck her knitting needles into my body . . ."

Lila bit her tongue. She wasn't crying but blocks of ice were melting inside of her. I told her that was all in the past. To forget it and go to sleep so she would arrive nice and fresh in New York where Henry was waiting for her. But I watched her wringing her fingers and knew she was tense, her jaws clenched, a knot in her stomach.

My poor Lila was seventy years old. And her life, peopled

with lovers and phantoms, was endlessly tormenting her. Seventy years old and not the slightest tear in which to drown her sorrows. Only words . . . She only had words to ease her soul. Words that didn't come naturally, that she had to search for, that she had to sort through and dredge up from the murky depths, that had remained imprisoned for ages. Bitter and pathetic words. Empty, insignificant words that had to be invested with truth, inflated with life. Words like birds that had to be lent wings and feelings to evoke love.

I was losing my footing. Amongst all the men she had known and loved, I didn't know which was her truly beloved. Hans, Henry, Gustave, Pierre, Marcel, her husband Frédéric, whose photographs papered the walls of her apartment and whom she had cherished up until his last day . . . They had each in turn played a role, left a shadow in her bed and a bruise on her heart . . . "Forever," Henry would have added. Lila closed her eyes. What man was filling her thoughts in that very instant?

And I wondered what I was doing there. Why had I entered Lila's world? Why hadn't I stayed in Paris, where, glued to the telephone, I would have waited for news from Lolo?

Knitting needles stuck into the body to abort . . .

I hadn't tried anything. As soon as I realized I was pregnant with Gino's child, I saw myself on his arm, in a wedding dress. But Gino preferred Marie. So I'd chosen France so Coraline wouldn't be ashamed of me. I'd gotten on the plane with my belly bound tight around my little Marcello. All because of Marie La Jalousie, Nitila's daughter . . .

11

"Sing hallelujah! Glory be to God! The Kingdom of Heaven is at hand!"

"Rejoice! Do not cry, child! For death is life and life is death!"

Those were the words that had been most vividly etched into Sybille's mind at her father Robert and her little brother's funeral. Perhaps because of the imperious way they had been hammered out. All the other words, mostly banalities quickly recited following smiles of brief compassion, had been sucked into the surrounding graves. As for the "sincere condolences," they had been transformed, on the path homeward, into Saint Cere Cordon Lantz! Saint Cere Cordon Lantz! Sincere Lantz! Of which she had ended up only retaining "Saint Lantz," once she had passed the threshold of mama Noémie's cabin.

For a long time after that, long after Noémie had taken her to see Judes and Coraline in Point-à-Pitre, Sybille believed that a certain Saint Lantz had accompanied her on that day. And in her evening prayers she would fervently repeat, "Saint Lantz! Pray for us poor sinners, for life is death and death is life! Saint Lantz, please give me back my father and my brother!" She was seven years old. It was the year 1961.

"Rejoice! Do not cry, for death is life and life is death!"

The creature that was in the habit of proffering that precept of hope was named Nitila. She took uncustomary pleasure in going around to Catholic and Protestant churches and cemeteries as well. As others would waltz from one dance to the next during the communal celebrations, sweating and drinking rum, following the Konga Typical band, Nitila flitted from one cabin to the next visiting the dead.

No sooner had agony, the dying, the last sacraments or extreme unction been mentioned, Nitila would spread her wings and alight, like a bird with long white feathers, at the side of grieving families. Without even paying her respects, she would walk in as if it were her house, go into the parlors and bedrooms, calculating with her eyes the number of candles and benches neatly lined up. She loved kissing the bodies freshly prepared for the viewing. Enjoyed following the vehicle carrying the deceased, walking in the procession amidst the flowers and wreaths to the rhythm of the funeral music. And then, at the trying moment of lowering the casket into the ground, which triggered the unleashing of cries, moans, the grinding of teeth, tears, trances, great heartbreak, oaths of eternal fidelity, and attempts at jumping into the grave, Nitila would deliver her message of hope.

"Rejoice! Do not cry! The Kingdom of Heaven is at hand! Rejoice, for death is life and life is death."

The first to arrive at a deathwatch, the first to sit down on the benches of the Catholic or Protestant churches, the last to present her condolences at the cemetery, and the last to leave, Nitila was forever dressed in white, ill-cut blouse, skirt pleated at the waist. A round fat little black woman of a rather comical appearance with bowed legs, Nitila was a person who nonetheless commanded respect. Though her words were curt, unchanging, recited without explanation, they were expressed in such a way that they became rooted in people's souls, remained stuck there as perfect truths and gave rise to mad hope. Dame Nitila seemed to hold the key to divine knowledge, the secret to a fountain at which only those who were not deceived by her ungracious appearance could drink.

Her voice imposed itself in an almost spectacular fashion. Not that it was very powerful, but because it echoed with calmness and restraint amidst the din of intermingling voices outraged in the face of death. Without shouting or cursing, Nitila reduced everyone to silence. The tears dried immediately. The cries became quiet sighs. Broken hearts were at once mended.

"Rejoice! Do not cry for life is death and death is life!"

At times some people would knit their incantations in with hers, repeating them until they became transfigured, until they no longer understood the meaning of their own words. Until, dazed, they would stumble and become lost in that laughter where life and death embrace like two old friends. Until they saw their resuscitated defunct reach the Kingdom of Heaven. The widows and orphans exclaimed, "Yes, that's him in flesh and blood, draped in white, a crown of orange blossoms on his head. He's holding a palm leaf and smiling at life." Then those who were living on earth would smile in turn and demand to die as quickly as possible, leave this sorrowful world of misery and torment.

"Do not cry, my brothers! For life is death and death is life."

Nitila didn't keep company with the living. She didn't visit the neighbors, didn't gossip, didn't mix with the black folk. She lived with her daughter Marie to whom she'd given birth at the age of thirteen after having been raped. The father, quickly unmasked, was the man known as Nérée, a senile maternal uncle of scandalous reputation who traded mint candies with his nephews and nieces for kisses in the underpants and promises of silence. In 1954, he'd stolen Nitila's virginity on one of his big binge nights at the Saint-Simoleon patronal celebration. Two days later, vomiting up his soul, his crime, and his guts in alcoholic vapors, he told Lisia, Nitila's mama, that the rum had been like a mad horse upon whose back a diabolical force had thrown and bound him. They had galloped and galloped from *morne* to *morne*, he not sobering, the horse not drinking or eating, traversing the ages and hours, nights and days, until they landed on the banks of his youth. That was how he found himself fifty years younger, two days before his marriage to his sweet Edmée, an Indian girl with long, silky black hair spilling over her shoulders who had sported the figure of a young girl all her life. He swore to Lisia that, in Nitila, he had recognized at one and the same time the odor, the forms, and even the voice of the late Edmée. She'd stuffed the piece of candy he offered her into her mouth. She had spread her thighs, and he had penetrated her, without harming her flesh, as if in a dream. Inside, another horse awaited him, already saddled, impatient, whinnying flames. The wild steed that spoke with an accent from beyond the grave predicted to him, "Nérée in three days, you will meet the horizon of life and the cliffs of death, hold on tightly to my neck!" Terrified, the old man had merely obeyed and believed—Lord he swore to it with all his soul—believed that Edmée was resuscitated. The laughter—Ha! Ha! Ha!—of the beloved woman knocked and bounced about in his heart. The long silken hair swept softly over her chest, the black tip of her little breasts grew stiff between his lips. And hungrily, with the teeth of a twenty-year-old, he sucked the milk of love with innocence a thousand times lost and suddenly reborn. In that other world, where the diabolical scum had led him, the uncle had seen the skin of his body become smooth, his flesh grow firm and his mind reappropriate the fine illusions of youth. Upon evoking that, he sobbed. Hypocritical tears, green contrition, groping about under his mattress for a rag. Nitila's mother dried his tears and listened to him all night long, holding his hands to assure him of her forgiveness, encouraging him to confess his crime down to the last filthy detail. Then, in the morning, while he was sleeping like a baby, she made an infusion for him that she put to his lips. A poisonous beverage, perfumed with cinnamon and well-sweetened, that in a flash, dug two deep hollows under the scoundrel's eyelids at the bottom of which his eyes—turned the color of rotten egg yolks—seemed for a very long time to be questioning Lisia.

No one asked Nitila about the father of her child. She revealed who the culprit was on the day Marie was born. The old uncle confessor was already no more than a bunch of bones devoured by earthworms underground in the cemetery when her water broke.

"The father!" she repeated, staring straight into the eyes of the elder woman who was delivering her. "He came on the night of Saint Simoleon's day. He was faceless. He appeared on a tall horse. He said, 'Life is death and death is life.'"

"Umph! Ass-backward . . ." groaned the matron after a brief silence. "And maybe the Good Lord's the devil! Water is fire, and heaven is earth . . . Everything is ass-backward, and you is a saint . . . Life is death and death is life! The things people say, Good Lord!"

Nitila emerged from childhood in the shadow of that citation and gave her breast to her little Marie while singing that obscure lullaby. Later she abandoned the Catholic religion, and one after the other became a Baptist, an Adventist, a Jehovah's witness, a Pentecostal evangelist, before creating her own church, which, she claimed, did not presumptuously lord over any land, was not built of stones, nor bricks, nor concrete. It rose up in people's hearts with the sole fervor of words and the supreme consolation that True Life began after life, for earthly existence was an endlessly recurring, dismal death.

For a long time, Nitila thought of Marie as a blessed little girl whose time on earth was counted. She listened to her breathing, hoping to pick up her lifeless body from the cradle any minute so that she might go back as quickly as possible to the other world, the True World. In the morning, she would disappointedly watch her awakening. When Marie had her fifth birthday, Nitila finally gave up hope. She dressed her daughter in white and ordained her Sister Marie of the Church of Saint-Simoleon.

Bearing the weight of that name, Marie never became an ordinary child. Neither angel nor demon, she seemed to be drifting between two extremes, between two absences, impalpable, immaterial, imperturbable, between heaven and hell, in a sinister purgatory in which disheveled, sodden souls were forever making their way up the same river in search of an improbable source. She was sly-eyed. Observed people stealthily. Hardly spoke.

People feared Marie from early on in her childhood. Not knowing how to explain her silence, depending on the day, people would chalk it up to something between mad hope and cruel disappointment—the two conflicting sentiments that always end up giving rise to one another. People believed she was educated, a book lover, who would naturally fulfill her destiny, when the time came, and take up her mama Nitila's calling. People thought she was hateful and jealous behind that bronze face of hers that, without a crease or a dimple, never showed the slightest quiver of emotion. People swore she was toxic, a traitor, like the species of deadly flowers in evening dresses, leaves fanned out and poisonous roots awaiting the fateful moment. People claimed she was vicious, inclined to the pleasures of the flesh. People nicknamed her Marie La Jalousie . . .

Marie and Sybille were the same age. When they were six, they shared the same first-grader bench in Grand-Saut, a division of Saint-Simoleon. They'd learned how to read with their voices chiming in together, to write using the same pen. The other little pickaninnies didn't go near Marie. The white voiles of Sister Marie of the Church of Saint-Simoleon kept them at a distance, petrified in a sort of fearful and mute respectation. As for the boys, they said she lured them into the thickets to let them suck on her *coucoune* that tasted of mint. Sybille found herself sitting next to Marie, who sharpened her black pencil, showed her the letter "*a*" before the school mistress did and offered her a piece of her bread topped with fried cod.

When Sybille's father died in Basse-Terre, in the cursed room of that Negress, Clothilde, the dream priestess and flower hauler, Marie was the only one who did not repeat the spiteful words that for days on end went back and forth from mouth to mouth, between Basse-Terre, Pointe-à-Pitre, and Saint-Simoleon, before being smeared across the front page of the daily paper, *Life in the Antilles* . . .

> *A married man and a well-known prostitute found dead*
> *in a cabin in Basse-Terre.*
> *Tragedy in Basse-Terre, death was lying in wait!*
> *Deadly rosebud.*
> *Murder or suicide. Poisoning or natural death?*
> *The suspected blood sausage proven to be innocuous.*

Why did she have a rosebud in her mouth?
Several neighbors have made important revelations.
They do not want to bear witness openly, but witchcraft
might be involved.
Mystery and mistrust hang over Basse-Terre.
The prostitute's cabin burned down during the night.

While perfidious and vulgar little ditties were being invented every day, flitting about like great black butterflies to scandalize-demoralize the chaste ears of young Sybille, Marie showed her silent but mature, attentive and serene friendship.

After her papa Robert and her little brother's funeral, Sybille never went anywhere without Marie. Thursday afternoons, while Nitila went running off to meet her dearly deceased and Noémie was wearing her knees down at the cemetery or else wandering the countryside looking for her lost love, the two little girls would get together. Get undressed. Marie tied a white ribbon around her neck. Put a red rosebud in her mouth. Then they would lie down side by side on a bed. Remain there for a very long time without moving or talking, their heads filled with blurry visions in which the headlines of *Life in the Antilles* were superposed with the songs of Saint-Simoleon's children and their own fantasies. Sometimes lurid scenes of the lovers' last hours unfolded in Marie's imagination, and she would fall into a sort of ecstasy. Her eyes and mouth became round with an "Oh!" that would wind up to a crescendo. "Oh! Oh! Oh! . . . They're here . . . Oh! Oh! Oh! . . ." And her body would grow strangely stiff before suddenly releasing and going limp.

When Marie would awaken, she never described what she'd seen. "There are no words," she assured. "No words for that . . ."

Sybille immediately allowed the vile little rhymes that related the story of her father and that girl Clothilde to come flooding into her mind . . .

'Twas blood sausage Robert had gone to fetch
A whore instead he did catch
Blood sausage hot!

Blood sausage cold!
The devil passed by that abode!

Blood sausage hot!
Blood sausage cold!
When a she-devil goes chewin on flowers
The dessert is the heart's last hour!

In 1963, two years after the double funeral, Noémie had half lost her mind. She wandered about, ethereal and regal, dignified, without knowing why anymore, wild-eyed, words as if unhinged. She just managed to gather up the last glimmers of reason in order to take Sybille to Pointe-à-Pitre and confide her to Coraline.

Before saying goodbye, Sybille and Marie lay down side by side, one last time, to relive the death of the lovers from Basse-Terre. They were only nine years old but promised each other to play out that scene over and over again until they died.

When Nitila passed away at the age of thirty-three, Marie was not yet twenty. Dressed entirely in white, she walked after her mama's casket past thousands of Christians, who, when the casket was lowered into the grave, chanted all at once:

"Rejoice, Nitila!
Oh no, do not cry, Marie!
For death is life
And life is death . . ."

Marie La Jalousie didn't even pretend to join in belting out Nitila's famous refrain. She smiled at no one, did not pronounce a single word, and kept her face fixed in a perfectly placid expression as long as the funeral lasted. Mouths kissed her, numbers of them: suction cup mouths, baby milk mouths, wet mouths, greasy red lipstick mouths, reciting, "Life is death, death is life." Handkerchiefs wiped her face, sweaty handkerchiefs, apron handkerchiefs, starched handkerchiefs, with large plaid, childish little flowers, and sparrows that declared over and over again, "life is death, death is life." Arms embraced her. Black, cacao, pale yellow hands. Dry fingers, crab-claw fingers. Gray fingernails, painted fingernails clawing the small of her back, pressing her neck.

Marie went back to her mama's shack unaccompanied. People watched her walking away in the distance, hoping it would not be long before she carried on with the dead woman's mission: flitting from cabin to cabin, leaving her message of hope, and nursing the flame that everyone now recognized was important, realizing unexpectedly that a whiff of wind could blow it out and that Nitila's death had left them at a loss, alone face to face with themselves. They suddenly became aware of that. Shaken, they discovered they were like a multitude of insignificant, inveterate cripples buffeted about in life's tempests. Despite their white hair, their stiff bones, and their jaded eyes, they were nothing. Subjugated by that child, Marie, they mourned Nitila's departure and found they had been devastated in one fell blow as had the Church of Saint-Simoleon, the cathedral Nitila had built for them, day after day, with the incense of words, the colors of dreams, and the vehemence of faith. So then they felt they had been betrayed and haltingly stammered out vapid words to quell their fever while a feeling of hate—bouquet of blood red wildflowers—was unfolding its petals in their hearts.

They waited for a long time.

A long time.

In the darkness of bedrooms, arms raised skyward, people faithfully repeated Nitila's Truth to themselves. "Life is death and death is life." Their eyes hurrying after the smoke of a five-cent candle, their mouths bitter with the pitiful prayers endlessly repeated; people searched everywhere for the breath of joy, the fire, the power and the glory of hope behind that worn couplet declaimed with all the fervor in their soul, but that they were always unable to lift up very high. Before even reaching the tin roofs, the Truth would fade out, become miserably frayed, leaving them stricken, thirsting, and exhausted. These demonstrations lacked Nitila's impressive charisma, her ringing voice to uphold that heavenly law that the ordinary humans of Saint-Simoleon knelt down to in times of old. Since then, cowardly skeptical choruses arose from deep within their bodies to denounce Nitila's unfounded church. Cry out that: Yes! Life did indeed flourish on this earth, whereas death was but ashes, rotting, and emptiness. As for Mamsell Marie La Jalousie, she might just as well go join her mother in the cemetery; not a soul would sing the canticles of the late Nitila for her.

In 1975, the following year, Marie was working as a salesgirl in a material store, Le Grand Palais. Sybille, a student nurse in her second year, had just started going out with Gino. When she saw Sybille outside the shop window, Marie hurried out onto the sidewalk and stood in front of her childhood friend.

"So! Did you continue?"

Sybille looked down, for she had never dared to play out the death of the lovers from Basse-Terre under Coraline's roof. Marie La Jalousie's face filled with pain. To win her forgiveness, Sybille recalled that from that moment on, she'd tried to renew the bonds that had brought them together back in Saint-Simoleon. She wanted to lash herself to Marie, never leave her again. She took no heed of the warnings, of the war that had been declared in her flesh. She scorned the voice of old Suzanne ordering her to get her hide into some hollow on the double, someplace Marie didn't know about. A thousand miles away, Lord! A thousand miles from Marie, far from the petrified face in which only the lips moved, like those of a marionette.

Lila smiled in her sleep. And while the hostess was announcing the landing, Sybille's thoughts turned—somewhat feverishly—to the wise people from back home, the ones who knew, the heralds of destiny to whom no one ever listened. They would suddenly pop up, spreading stories, ranting on about their predictions, linking events to one another before they had even become clearly defined elements of a coherent story, laden with sighs and sudden new developments, long before the accumulation of facts brought out the basic storyline and the red herrings, unmasked the demons.

In 1969, Sybille was fifteen years old; Suzanne, an old cane-cutter from Saint-Simoleon sat down in a bamboo armchair in Coraline's living room. She'd come to Pointe-à-Pitre to explain how, in a dream, she'd seen Marie La Jalousie come into the world with the blessing of Gloria's daughters—three sisters—who had been carted away in the Grand-Saut River the same year as her birth. Three poor virgins thirsting for love, lecherous hearts, treacherous souls wandering in purgatory. It happened on the big laundry day. Standing in the water up to their thighs, heads tied up, and blouses soaked, they were laughing and chatting about their future love lives. Now that's how a body goes about seeking out death around that side of the sea! As two and two make four, the all-too-clear ring of their laughter loosed the anger of some Satan Lucifer who was surveying his territories along the river bank. The waters began to roar and swell stealthily. In no time at all, they'd been caught up, tossed about, cast from rock to rock, dashed to pieces. Realizing their life was coming to an end in the raging and muddy waters of the Grand-Saut, they had obtained from heaven the respite of only a tiny prayer, an "Ave Maria." Their bodies were found three days later, throats filled with leaves, splintered bones sticking through the bruised flesh. *Titiri*-minnows seething in their eye sockets. And branches tangling in their hair, plaited into wild braids by the fingers of the current.

Over in the Middle Kingdom, far from heaven and two steps from hell, moaned the ancestor, and there, the three sisters encountered old Nérée . . . The scoundrel, the uncle who had raped Nitila. It was the very day of his own decease. Upon a wretched nag he rode, twisting with pain, his mouth and entrails burning with Lisia's poison. And he was weeping, that dirty dog! Imploring those who crossed his path, "Pray for me, my brothers and sisters! Pray for my soul! For rum ran my life amok. Because of it, I rammed my niece, Nitila. And the child to be born will have no papa."

That is how the three love-starved virgins got hitched onto Marie. Even before her birth, the child had inherited three living-dead godmothers, dregs of the bad waters, shady, glassy-eyed females, balsam-wood bodies that echo-rumbled around in a racket multiplied a thousand times over. And Lord, did those virgins sob over their interrupted lives and the passions they missed! Like ticks that latch onto a cow, they lived at Marie's expense, their teeth sunk into her heart, sucking her life away through the pores, feeding on her dead skin, her fingernail clippings, discarded combings. They were behind the child's every thought, breath, and dream. They saw through Marie's eyes, envying with three voices anything that had any resemblance to a fleshly thrill.

And while Nitila ran from one cemetery to the next, repeating her Truth about life and death, the three virgins were humming to Marie that love alone was life's daily bread.

Sybille sighed at the thought of that old mulatta-*chabine* with yellow dentures who'd related that somber story to her. Certainly she was already dead now too, had joined the others . . .

Though she was torn between times past and those to come, between New York, Pointe-à Pitre, and Paris, cramped up in the seat of the airplane, Sybille was feeling almost whole again for the first time since she'd fled Guadeloupe. After Marcello's departure, which had followed the unfortunate encounter with Marie on the platform of the Raspail Metro Station, she'd thought she was lost, condemned to grow old and bitter, bowed down with shame, and hopelessly stuck in the lies upon which her life had been built.

Sybille recalled having shuddered when Suzanne finished relating the tale of the three sisters. Coraline had listened without saying a word. Remained silent for a long time after the end.

Then she'd burst out, "Dreams! More dreams! Dear Lord! People in Guadeloupe are always coming up with the latest dream to explore or interpret. A dream held up like a lantern to light our days!"

Tapping her fingers on the arms of her easy chair, Suzanne had chuckled, "Yes indeed! I come up from Saint Simoleon for that reason alone. My back is constant torment, my knees true punishment. I nearly blind. I just missed falling flat on my face while getting on the bus. And I here all the same . . . I don't have the gift. I never prayed for that. But it came to me. I ain't been to the Pointe for five centuries. So there you have it, that's the way it is. I used to run into old Nérée and his niece Nitila from time to time. I watched how Marie La Jalousie pursued your Sybille. Like a fly around honey-syrup. At the funeral of her poor papa Robert and her little brother, I noticed the way Marie was looking at her while Nitila was declaiming her Truth. Cora, this ain't the first time this dream has visited me. And believe me, I went round and round a hundred times before making up my mind, especially since it resuscitated that unfortunate girl, Clothilde, the dreamer-flower gatherer. I ain't here in front of you, my dear Cora, of my own will. It's that I couldn't back up no more. I don't know nothing about Clothilde, but I'm sure that she the one pushing me. Every evening she comes with that rosebud between her teeth and little wings sticking out of her back. She swears she wants to help Sybille. Robert and her are lovers in paradise. Death was their destiny . . . But Clothilde's suffering. She's miserable thinking a defenseless orphan girl's been abandoned to the claws of jealousy."

Coraline sighed, "Good Lord! Sweet Jesus! Just leave the dead good and well amongst themselves!"

"I've done my duty, Cora. Sybille has already lost her father and little brother, her mama's in the asylum. And Marie ain't done with her work yet! She'll be on her heels for a long time, to make off with whatever she can, Cora, you know Jealousy . . ."

"Keep quiet, *chabine*! God Almighty! What are you trying to put into this child's head?" shouted Coraline.

"Fine, I going back to Saint-Simoleon," the visitor had grumbled with the satisfied air of having carried out her duty. Then, taking from her purse a tiny bottle of pinkish liquid that she set down on the living room table, she murmured two words to Coraline, who immediately stuck the vial into her corsage. And no one ever heard speak of Suzanne, the three love-starved virgins, and Marie La Jalousie again.

•••

In 1975, Gino was at the height of his glory. Sybille had just recently authorized him to slip a finger into her panties. Gino was a stretcher bearer at the general hospital in Pointe-à-Pitre where she was studying to be a nurse. At the age of thirty-two, the single gigolo was a true connoisseur of women. Sometimes he pretended to be a young doctor just out of school from Toulouse or Bordeaux and would, in no time, snare the naïve young birds in whites, who, without missing a step, followed him into that game in which it's always difficult to distinguish giving from taking.

When Marie caught a glimpse of Sybille outside the window of the Grand Palais, she was walking on Gino's arm. She introduced them to each other. In those days, Marie measured cloth by the meter glancing jealously at couples of lovers going by on the sidewalk. She had smooth skin, straightened hair, pulled back. Her lips, which had already kissed more than one man, were painted with dark red lipstick. The two friends had exchanged addresses, and the following week, Marie was stretching her body out in Gino's bed.

It was an afternoon in the dry season. Sybille had finally made up her mind to offer her body to Gino. Timid and a little sweaty, she rapped at his door. Three quick little taps, heralding the long declarations of love knotted in her flesh, "Here I am. I belong to you till the end of time. I'm yours, Gino. But, please don't hurt me. I'm entrusting you with my treasure so that you'll finally give up the other girls you love less than me . . ."

On the other side of the wall, the bedsprings squeaked. Then silence. Sybille had gone down into the street, had waited over an hour, alone with her own breathing, posted at the corner of a gift store. Gino and Marie came out late, one after the other, like a couple of thieves.

The next day, as if nothing had happened, Gino had once again declared his love to Sybille. He was pushing an old body with large feet in a wheelchair.

"You the one I going to marry, sweet Sybille. You the only one who . . ."

"Meet me at five o'clock in front of the photographer's, Place de la Victoire. We'll go to your room."

Gino had swallowed hard and cast a wink at the old man who was drooling in the chair.

Sybille had let those words out not really understanding where they might have come from. They'd been running through her mind all day long . . . We'll go to your room . . . We'll go to your room . . . We'll go to your room. And while she was learning how to count the drops from the perfusion, she pictured herself lying under Gino, incapable of uttering a single word, incapable of relaxing her stiff body . . . We'll go to your room . . . We'll go to your room . . . And she was seeing the horror in Coraline's face, her eyes glaring at her in silent reprobation from an imaginary portrait hanging on the wall in Gino's room. Several times, Gino had appeared through the blinds on the classroom door, throwing her kisses that unleashed giggling and chattering amongst the students.

Pointe-à-Pitre was beginning to close up shop when she reached their meeting place. Gino was already waiting for her, a cigarette hanging from his lips.

"Gino, I'm afraid," she mumbled.

"Sweetheart, do you love me? That's the only question. Are you prepared to live by the side of the man you love? I'm sure of myself, Sybille. You the only girl who counts. I've already told you, the others are just a pastime. I've been waiting for you for two years now, isn't that right, honey?"

" . . . "

"You know what's in my heart, eh? Let's go!" Gino took her hand. "We'll get married, we'll have children, lots of children. As many as you want . . ."

"You promise you'll marry me, Gino?"

"You know I will!"

"And if we have a son, we'll name him Marcello!"

Gino laughed and sang out three notes . . . Marcello o-o. Marcello o-o, life you will know ow-ow!

"So you agree, Marcello!"

He laughed again and shook his head, "Whatever you want!"

"I'm afraid, Gino!"

"A woman ought not tremble when she giving her flower to the man she loves . . . But maybe you don't love me enough, Sybille? So if that's the case, we'd best call it quits right now. Don't force yourself!"

"No, don't get mad! I love you . . ."

"Are you going to prove it to me, sweet honey?"

She closed her eyes and answered, "Yes, Gino . . ."

An unconditional yes to love. Yes to the one-way trip into doubt and torment. Yes to the risk of a belly on credit . . . Yes to spells being cast, to jealousy nesting within her like a swarm of snakes.

Gino's place was a gloomy room furnished with a wrought-iron bed covered with wrinkled grayish sheets. Open like a mouth hungry for the fresh flesh of the Negresses Gino brought home. There was dust on the shelves and rust on the fridge. A door left ajar opened onto a niche fitted with a sink filled with dirty dishes. Draped over refundable bottles, a floor cloth full of holes was in the process of drying.

At first they sat on the bed. While Gino's long hands came and went over her body, Sybille thought of Marie. She pictured her back when the two of them used to mime the last moments of the lovers from Basse-Terre. Marie, stretched out naked on her mama's bed, swearing there were no words to describe what she had seen, only those repeated oh's!

A little rhyme came back to her too . . .

'Twas blood sausage Robert had gone to fetch
A whore instead he did catch
Blood sausage hot!
Blood sausage cold!
The devil passed by that abode!

When Gino had finished undressing her, Sybille felt as if she were seven years old again, naked under Marie's gaze. Marie, whose presence she could still feel under Gino's fingers, in his hair, in the smell of the sheets. Past and present overlapped . . .

Blood sausage hot!
Blood sausage cold!
Death passed by that abode!

In the old days, their running into one another had always seemed innocent, simply strokes or snags of luck. But eighteen years later, when Sybille ran into Marie again in Paris, where so many people jostle up against one another without seeing each other, live together without their eyes ever meeting, seeking out, or gauging one another, the past had suddenly sprang back up, ripped off its mask theatrically.

"Oh! Oh!" Those same oh's that Marie cried out at the age of seven to express things that were emerging but that she wasn't able to put words to.

Marie had shouted, "Oh! Oh! Oh!" into the crowd. And her voice had shot straight over to Sybille making her start.

"Oh! Sybille! It's really you . . . What a miracle!" To draw nearer to Sybille, Marie had made her way through the crowd, pushing aside the commuters thronging on the platform.

"M'ma, who's that?" Marcello had asked. "Who is that lady?"

"It's nothing! Someone I knew in the West Indies."

"Oh! Oh! Sybille! Sister!" roared Marie shaking the abundant mane of hair, weaved with false extensions, which undulated on either side of her face.

"Oh! It's a miracle! After all this time! It can't be true, Sybille! God has answered my prayers. I've found you at last . . ."

And she had started unwinding reels and reels of words like a mad woman inhabited by a long-winded spirit . . . Her life in Guadeloupe since Sybille had left, her infertility, her religious crises, the construction of her house . . . She was now living with an African she'd met in Basse-Terre, a cloth merchant who traded between Pointe-à-Pitre and Dakar. This was the first time she was traveling with him. They were, in a manner of speaking, in transit in France. Oh! What a miracle! Isn't it, Sybille?"

Sybille was praying above all that Marie wouldn't pronounce Gino's name. Thoughts nesting one into the other, she was considering fleeing as a last recourse. Run, far from Marie. Quick!

Shield Lolo from her revelations.

"Ah! So this is Gino's son!" she exclaimed forcing a kiss on Marcello. "A big boy! I'm sure his papa is proud of him . . . Ah! I'm so happy for you, Sybille!"

In 1975, Marie didn't have all that fake hair. She didn't use words with so much passion. She gave her body to Gino. She spent her time in his bed . . .

With no sense of decency, without the slightest regret, Marie had the gall to bring up Gino, gazing sharply at Marcello, like an eagle at its prey. Eighteen years later . . .

"Oh! he's the spitting image of his father! By the way, I ran into him last week. We talked about you, about our youth."

Then Sybille saw Marcello's face slowly discomposing. While Marie was pouring out those fateful couplets in a monotone voice, he had looked at her as if she were simply monstrous.

"Oh! So you haven't heard? Why is that? Well he's settled down. Married. A good father. He's been preaching at the Protestant church for going on . . ."

Bits of incisive sentences that awakened the past and suddenly generated a father for Marcello.

"He's the very portrait of Gino. A fine-looking boy. And nice, that's for sure . . . Your son should get to know him . . ."

When the two women separated, Marcello didn't say a word. He disappeared into the crowd, leaving her alone.

12

At the John Fitzgerald Kennedy airport, Henry was waiting for us in the company of James-Lee.

For seventy-four years of age, Henry was definitely attractive. A strong upright man like a tree full of sap, old and green at the same time. Lila hadn't exaggerated; he did look like Harry Belafonte. His hair was a shiny black. His face, barely wrinkled, bore several spots that were darker brown than the rest of his skin, the color of dried banana leaves. When he wrapped his arms around Lila he lifted her up and swung her around like a child, I immediately imagined them fifty years earlier in postwar Paris just as she'd described it to me so many times. I feared for Lila's heart, but Henry had two large velvety hands that were endlessly caressing her. Lila laughed, cried, let out little yelps of protest. While James-Lee watched them from behind his dark glasses, with a thin smile espoused by a dense gray mustache scattered with white hairs, I was telling myself that if I'd had the chance of meeting someone like Henry, I would have never let him go. I would have said good-bye to France. I would have sold everything in Paris. I would have become an American. I could never have lived far from his arms, from his long hands . . .

Seventy-four years old and his gaze was lit with such a powerful light that it was almost blinding. In Henry's eyes, where little white clouds floated, I suddenly saw my own reflection, with my bumps and dents. I discovered myself as I truly was, loveless, dried up, lost, abandoned, alone, and miserable. I envied him, so elderly, so serene, not even cracked by the blows of life, happy.

James-Lee had a much lighter complexion than Henry's. I remember having deduced that his mother, Lana, must have been a mulattress. A pretty mulattress from Barbados, for James-Lee was a very handsome man. When he shook my hand, I felt a strange thrill in my heart that left me in a momentary state of confusion before it suddenly forced me to give love a try, take my life by the scruff of the neck.

Henry and James-Lee invited us to The Kreyol restaurant. Henry owned a green Buick dating back to the seventies. He'd put a heart-shaped sticker on the windshield: *God loves you! But don't forget to love yourself!* The seats, with brand new striped seat covers, were hidden under myriads of cushions adorned with pompoms that Lana had made throughout her lifetime. Even during her illness, she'd continued to wind all colors of wool around cardboard cutouts, knot the strings and make pompoms. As the cancer gradually spread through her body, ate into her lungs, she started making them smaller and smaller.

"This is the last one she finished," explained Henry in his smooth French, brushing his fingers over a yellow, slightly grimy cushion. "Twenty-three years since she left us . . . When she made her pompoms she'd always say, 'Oh, it's quite a job! Real hard work!' And I would answer, 'But, those cushions of yours are of no use!' And then she'd retort, 'Yes they are, they keep my hands and my mind busy. And they take up time. *Time goes away . . .*'" he laughed at those last words.

James-Lee was driving in a very laid back way. His eyes went slipping from the road to his rearview mirror where Lila was reflected. I was behind him, I could see his neck, his square cut curly black hair, the top of his head, and his two small ears. That was when I felt like putting my hand into his shirt collar and kissing his neck. I was in New York, and I was just blown over by the feeling of giddiness the city induced, by everything that was rushing past my eyes. Excited at being in that car whose driver couldn't possibly imagine the awakening desire that was running through my body. He hadn't uttered a word of French since the airport. At times, Henry would translate something he said . . . "Oh, James-Lee suggests you take a look at the Twin Towers! That's Central Park . . . We're crossing Broadway . . ."

I'd never been anywhere but Guadeloupe and Paris. I told myself I was in that feverish giddy state of mind because of the tall buildings and the English signs, all those American flags waving on the fronts of the skyscrapers, the hum of the city too. Because of the clouds that seemed to scud through the sky faster than in Paris. Because of the hundreds of pompoms piled up on the seats of the Buick. Maybe because of Lila who was laughing and clapping at New York, the memories of Paris, and her faraway youth in Henry's eyes. As we were driving toward the restaurant, I caught myself thinking how good it must feel to be in James-Lee's arms, laying one's head against his chest, naked, under the same sheet. And at the same time those absurd ideas were growing larger in my mind, certain knots were beginning to loosen: I was no longer afraid for Marcello. I wasn't thinking about what had become of Gino anymore. And those lies of mine that had been laid bare no longer cast shadows over me. I suddenly felt liberated. Free and ecstatic. Thrown into a new world, far far away from the deaths in my childhood.

Instead of touching James-Lee's neck, I sought out Lila's hands that she had clasped together between her thighs, on her blue and white pleated skirt. Her little hands covered with age spots and deformed with arthritis. I found the hard bones of her fingers with long nails painted Shalimar red. Then I closed my eyes so I couldn't see James-Lee's neck or his dark glasses in the rearview mirror any more. And I confidently allowed myself to be led like a blind person through the racket of the streets, Lila and Henry's laughter, and the sentences that James-Lee was pronouncing in English.

I saw New York
New York USA
I never saw nothin, aye
I never saw nothin, aye so high

Aye, It's high, New York!
New York USA

Empire State Building, aye, it's high!
Rockefeller Center, aye, it's high!
International Building, aye, it's high!

When the car stopped, I was as dazed as if I'd just gotten off ten rounds of the Ferris wheel at the Foire du Trône. We parked the car in a lot. The employee, an old, slightly hunchbacked white man just grumbled and exchanged a ticket for a bank note that he incorporated into wads of five, ten, and twenty-dollar bills.

"So, Lila! We're not far now!" whispered Henry. "Tell me if you're feeling tired . . ."

"Not at all! I'm in great shape!"

"Lean on my and James-Lee's arm all the same! I know you, eh? Still so *fière*, eh? So proud . . ."

As for me, it was as if I were walking on moss. I felt as if I were floating. My heart was beating harder than a drum to the tune of Gainsbourg's couplets.

I never saw nothin, aye
I never saw nothin aye so high
Aye, It's high, New York!
New York USA

As soon as we stepped into the restaurant, James-Lee hurried behind the counter. Henry and Lila sat down at a table. There were around ten of them, set with paper table settings decorated with coconut trees and tropical fruit. On the walls, Haitian paintings depicting women's faces with white handkerchiefs on their heads who seemed to look upon the world with a severe glare. Other paintings offered the inevitable landscapes of white sandy beaches, windswept islands, and setting suns. And there was a series of portraits with captions . . . Henry at twenty-five. Henry at sixty. Henry and Lana in front of the first Kreyol Food. Lana, pregnant. The children at all ages. Sundra looked like her mother. There she was on graduation day at the University. Michael in front of a computer. Rodgers standing outside his garage. Sundra and Michael on Thanksgiving Day. James-Lee at ten. James-Lee at thirty, the day of his wedding. James-Lee married . . . Somewhat sobered, I went to lean on my elbows at the counter, so as not to bother Lila and Henry, who, fingers entwined on their table, were whispering secrets into each other's ears. I stood in admiration of them, a black man and a white woman who had shared in a love affair during the postwar years and who'd decided to meet back up in New York almost fifty years later. After a little while, Lila shed a tear. Henry immediately held out a handkerchief. Wiped her cheeks.

"Don't worry about it, baby!"

"You know, I regretted it . . ."

"Forget about regrets. You're here now, and that's what counts."

"You held it against me, eh?" said Lila worriedly.

Henry burst out laughing.

"Damn right! I even prayed you'd die as soon as I left."

Lila scoffed, bittersweet, "Don't worry, it won't be long now."

"Please don't think about those things!" begged Henry pushing back his chair. "I'll show you the pictures . . . Hey! Do you still like jazz, Lila? Listen, it's Miles, 'Someday My Prince Will Come,'" he went on pointing with his finger as if the music were a butterfly or a bird, a living body endowed with form and color.

Lila and I ended up alone together. We didn't have anything to say to one another; we would sit around remembering the men who'd crossed our paths. For her, Henry, Hans, and Frédéric and a few of the others. As for me, I would recollect being back in Guadeloupe with Gino. Hanging on Gino's arm at Place de la Victoire. At La Renaissance movie theater, watching a karate film because Gino was a Bruce Lee fan. I didn't really care for those kinds of films, but I followed him around like a little dog on our rare outings. Mostly to his room . . . I had given him my lips and opened my legs to please him. To be like my rivals.

How old was I . . .twenty-one? He'd been running after me for two years. He swore that apart from me, girls were nothing:

perverted sluts. He was waiting to pick my flower before leaving them to their indignity. He was skillful with words and little by little, all the girls ended up giving in to him. We believed him. We persuaded ourselves that words had the power of changing destiny. We were convinced that words were feelings drawn straight from the heart, with no makeup or costumes. We'd get bogged down in his lovely prose. That's why I had Marcello, because of words.

In Paris I'd known Patrick from Brittany, Michel from Corsica, and Daniel from Martinique. Tepid and rocky love affairs that didn't give me the fever, didn't bruise me, and left me disillusioned. It was because I'd been around them so much, dated them, listened to their propositions, and rubbed up against them that I forced myself to believe in possible paradises built on the words *Love* and *Forever*. Words that I would catch in my mouth after them and suck right down to the soul like apple-mangos, trying to detect the taste of flowers, rum, or vanilla.

I was nearing forty years of age; it was the year 1993, seven years before 2000. And for the first time, I was wildly attracted to a man entirely of my own volition. James-Lee . . . And I hadn't even seen his eyes yet. We had shaken hands. We hadn't spoken to each other. But I'd felt the desire to run my fingers through his hair, stroke his neck. Push his head between my legs. He was married . . .

I felt younger, drunk on desire and determined to do mad things, write love letters, throw myself to my knees in front of him. I was burning to go into the back courtyard. To put my arms around his waist. But I remained well behaved, didn't move. So afraid of acting ridiculous.

Henry came back with three photo albums. He sat down next to Lila and asked me to come over. James-Lee joined us. He was standing near me. His warm breath blowing gently down my neck.

13

Marcello!

Sybille had named him after her brother.

Her sadly missed younger brother.

Marcello . . . to get even with fate for having robbed her of the brother that Noémie's belly had promised.

Marcello to pretend that the hours whiled away with Gino had been nothing but a dream. As if the child had come into her life through the workings of the Holy Ghost, a fine magic trick . . .

Marcello to rub out of her mind the idea that she had only been one out of so many others in Gino's heart.

Marcello to cleanse herself of Gino, erase him from her memory . . .

"Your papa? He's in heaven, Marcello!"

"Your poor papa, he's dead! Everyone in Guadeloupe lamented his depart."

"No, I don't have any photos! You know back in those days, people didn't take many photographs."

"No! It's no use to go back to Guadeloupe. My parents are dead and so is your papa. Luckily we've got our Lila!"

And Marcello would listen to her, swallow her lies. Poor innocent child sunk in fairy tales. He was maybe about five years old when he asked after his father the first time. Because of the children in kindergarten bragging about their fathers, threatening to go tell things to their fathers who existed somewhere in a world that Marcello had a hard time imagining. Papas who were always saviors, who suddenly appeared out of nowhere, like giant, avenging eagles. Papas full of courage, who feared no one, not even the school mistress. So when the little boys uttered the word *papa*, Marcello promptly felt inferior to his comrades, almost crippled. Having only his two lone mothers to present to the warlike world of recreations, he would lose all the battles before they even began, unnerved and defeated from the outset.

Death had imposed itself upon Sybille's lips. Death to justify the absence of a father, to close that chapter. A legend which evoked only silence.

"Your papa's no longer alive!"

And there was nothing more to be said.

"Killed . . . in a car accident . . . and buried."

"I don't want to talk about it. It's too painful to think about. Don't ask me any more questions, please . . ."

Up until the age of twelve, as he grew up cramped in between Sybille and Lila, Marcello was forever harassing his mother to describe his father, paint a face, hang feelings on him, and, above all, invent a destiny for him.

"How did he die?"

"In a car accident, I've told you that a hundred times . . ."

"When did he die?"

"Just before you were born. We were going to be married."

"What was he like?"

"Oh, so very kind . . . so . . ."

"And is his mother still in Guadeloupe?"

"No! She's not alive anymore! They're all dead! Oh, don't think about that anymore, my little Lolo! We're just fine here in France with our dear Lila, aren't we? Forget about Guadeloupe . . ."

And no matter how skillfully the two women were at fencing, at filling up rooms with their litanies and their gestures, buttering him up with caresses and wetting him with kisses, and also smothering him with presents, with conspired surprises and silly nicknames, Marcello was forever harping back on that dead father of his.

Throughout those long years, Sybille had gradually given in to Marcello's constant pressuring. She'd made Gino look wonderful. An exceptional father. Tragic death. The love of a lifetime . . . Flames would kindle in Marcello's eyes. And at times, looking at her son, Sybille—who told her stories in a sparing, mechanical manner—ended up believing in her own fabrications, seeing Gino lying in a casket.

Everything had gone awry in his thirteenth year. Classmates of his, West Indians born in Paris as he was, had come back completely smitten with Guadeloupe. So then Marcello begged his mother to take him there on the next vacation. Sybille sent him to London to learn English.

She'd lost her temper, "But I keep telling you, there's nothing but corpses there!"

"That doesn't matter! We'll go swimming! You can show me your school . . ."

"What for? What do you want to go stirring up over there, Marcello? Don't you understand it would cause me too much pain? You want to make me suffer? You want me to cry? Aren't you happy here with me and your good mama Lila . . .

"And anyway, there's too much jealousy over there! Witchcraft! Don't let yourself get hoodwinked by the images of paradise that you see on television. One day, when you're older, I'll tell you how Guadeloupe almost killed me too. There are witches over there that poison innocent people, untie marriage knots, and make shops go bankrupt . . . I lost my mama, I lost my papa because of that jealousy. All I have left are my old adoptive parents, Judes and Coraline . . .

"Come on, forget about Guadeloupe, my little Lolo!"

So then Marcello started closing himself up in silence.

Thinking.

Dreaming about Guadeloupe where his dead father lay at rest and some secret that his mother refused to share.

He kept quiet, ruminating over whole strings of questions that obsessed him about his father, his country, and death.

He kept quiet when the two women held discussions about men over his head, as if he were nothing but a cushion shaped like a little boy set down on the sofa.

He kept quiet when Lila swore she loved black folk and when she forced him to look at the photo of her Henry "*Faut rêver*," when she hugged him tight in her arms, whispering to him that he was her blessed little boy.

He listened. Obeyed. Docilely conformed to the clichés of the model little boy that they imposed on him.

So as not to displease them, he raised his eyes, diligently searched for the phantoms that his mama Lila was on the lookout for on the roof of the building across the street. People that were getting on buses and trains. And who went tumbling down one after the other.

He was very well behaved between his two mothers. Silent little bird, swathed in their chitchat, coddled with their love.

Marcello was thirteen. But they hadn't seen him grow up. And they thought he didn't express himself enough, didn't laugh enough, didn't eat enough.

"Eat Lolo! To put on weight!"

"Come here, Lolo, I want a kiss!"

"Say good morning, Lolo!"

They kissed him as if they wanted to devour him. Spoiled him. Baby toys. Presents for no particular reason, just to receive a thank you, demand hugs, and force him to grimace with smiles. They gave him everything he wanted. Everything except Guadeloupe, which he had secretly promised to himself.

One day, he didn't want any more of their kisses, didn't want them to touch him anymore. He was sixteen; he was in love with a young black girl from Sarcelles who had the right to smooch on him, cuddle him, who braided his hair for him.

"I'm too old for that now!"

He'd gotten too old for everything. Too old for Lila and Sybille. Too old for their love, their jealous kisses, their Lolo this, Lolo that.

"Call me Marcello! I'm sick of your Lolos!"

Nights I lay awake in my bed. I pictured Gino accusing me of burying him alive. Marcello looked at me as if I were a stranger. He was walking along between Marie and Gino, calling them

Mama and Papa. I found myself in a sort of cage along with Lila. We were locked inside. We were pecking at the bars with our beaks. We were crying out, but no one opened the door for us.

Some mornings I got up thinking I would tell Marcello everything. To free myself of my lies. I'd go over the sentences several times in my mind . . .

"Sit down, Marcello. You're sixteen now. You're nearly an adult. I have to tell you some things about your father and myself. About your birth . . . Your father isn't dead. He's living in Guadeloupe. I thought I was doing the right thing . . . I was young, try to understand . . . I was so hurt when he abandoned me. So I wanted to wipe him out of our lives . . . Don't worry, Lolo, one day we'll go see that Guadeloupe of yours . . ."

But the months slipped by, my getting cold feet as soon as Marcello appeared, suddenly seeming so lanky to me, so incredibly imposing. I didn't have time to say those words. We met Marie La Jalousie on the platform of the Raspail Station . . .

Guadeloupe. Sybille didn't think she would go back there anytime soon. What for? To go visit the cemetery and kneel down before three graves? And gratify Marcello, in having a semblance of a conversation with Gino? Hash over the good old days?

Gino was now an upright family man. Ever since he'd married a girl of the evangelist religion, he'd stopped chasing after women, Marie La Jalousie had claimed. He adored only Jesus Christ who died on the cross for the sins of mankind. He even preached at the Protestant church, that handsome Gino . . .

What had become of the thousands of vows of love he used to recite so skillfully? Perhaps he'd put them all away in a padlocked chest and then thrown them into the sea, along with the memories of all the women he'd cheated on.

"Do you love me, Gino?" Sybille would implore.

"You know I do. Get undressed!"

"And Marie?"

"She doesn't count . . . Don't dirty your lips with that *manawa*-whore!"

"Why do you go with her then?"

"It doesn't count! Come closer!"

"And when are we going to be married, Gino?"

"Stop asking questions, Sybille. Get undressed and come closer . . . Be quiet and kiss me!"

To meet up with Gino for those hasty embraces, Sybille would lie to Coraline, pretending she was studying with schoolmates.

Twice a week, he awaited her in his bed, already naked under the sheets. Didn't answer her greeting. Smiled voraciously at her figure. Then, eyes closed, sure of himself, he held out his arms like an actor in a bad French film, so that she would quickly come to his arms, and be nothing but the body he so desired. All he wanted from her were the motions of lovemaking that he ordered her to execute. Though he would groan a few syrupy and vapid words, he hardly ever talked about himself and was reluctant to use the suave phrases that had led Sybille into his bed. He loved giving orders.

"Kiss me!"

"Get undressed!"

"Come here!"

"Lie down here!"

He lived for his pleasure alone.

"Spread your legs!"

"Open up!"

"Put me in!"

At the time, Sybille was twenty-one years old. She had very little sexual experience. Had let boys in her class touch her once or twice. She had grown up sheltered from the facts of life among Judes, Coraline, and Anne-Lise, the servant. Protected. Never alone. Surrounded by her family. Loved. The pride and joy of Judes and Coraline . . . Sisi this! Sisi that! . . .

When she would worry about not being engaged, married, or a mother yet, Coraline recommended patience. "You have your whole life to find a husband. You are gifted with rare beauty, my little Sisi."

Dark, tall, with a fine upright carriage like that of her mother Noémie, Sybille had lustrous skin, thick hair. And her eyes were sketched in charcoal. She felt it was a flaw that she had not yet partaken of a man's flesh, for most of the girls her age had already dabbled in it. At times, she recalled herself at seven, lying next to Marie La Jalousie, miming. Horrid visions that she suppressed, fearing some curse would be called down upon her, would awaken the madness that had taken seed in Noémie's soul.

She'd given herself to Gino for all those reasons. And especially to taste the fruit that everyone hungered after, that had killed her poor papa Robert.

Gino had murmured to her: "I'm going to teach you how to make love . . ."

He'd pushed her into his bed. Had lain down on her. Had hurried her, mumbling that he loved her, moaning, "It feels good, don't it?"

And then suddenly he'd let out a cry, as if some demonic spirit had shaken him from inside, yanked itself out of his body, freed itself from his entrails, to penetrate into Sybille's body, shoot through her in a flash.

So that was what love was? Hasty gestures. The feeling of something left unfinished. Tearing, sighing, deliverance . . .

So that's what it was? Using the salt and the water of your flesh, the pain and the giving of your body to produce love. That's what making love was? . . . Helping a man expel the monster that crouched within him.

So, to come to Gino's aid, she forced herself to moan in echo to his plaints. To move her hips to sustain his cadence. To open herself up and spread herself wide. Proud and surprised at the same time to be there, in that bed, under a man who needed her body in order to exist and rid himself of the hideous creatures that inhabited him.

She thought, so that was what a woman's mission on earth was! And then, when it was all over with—the demons vanished—to forget that she had been a witness to his dependence. Feign blindness. Pour oneself into the mold of the submissive damozel while he took his male postures back on.

At times, Gino was just like a frightened child. Sybille would immediately wrap her arms around him, like a mother protecting her firstborn. She accorded him the haven of her breast and the eternity of her heart. She murmured words of love to him that for a longtime sought refuge somewhere inside of him and that, if he wasn't careful, seeped into his flesh. But he was always able to shoo them away like black birds as soon as he'd rid himself of his demons. Tender and sad words, reflecting her own thoughts that went flitting from Marie to Gino, from Robert to Clothilde . . .

Blood sausage hot
Blood sausage cold
When a she-devil goes chewin on flowers
The dessert is the heart's last hour . . .

Soon Gino would grant no more time for even the smallest caress, the skimpiest tender word. All he could do was keep repeating, "It feels good, don't it? So good!" as if he were making sure the pleasure was shared. She was his object that he would overpower and mount like a swine. She was the dry trail that led to his sexual pleasure. A rocky land over which he endlessly strode, at one and the same time prospector, dowser, and explosives expert. Impatient to find the gold, the fire, and the salty water. Gold veins, torrents, and trickles of water that he drank in with the same thirst. He became a hard rock upon Sybille's body. Banged up against her until she turned to stone. Two stones worn down from rubbing together to kindle the fire that would liberate his soul.

"Oh, Gino," she implored. "Tell me how much you love me!"

"Be quiet, Sybille! It's better being here like this, with no words . . ."

"What about Marie?"

"Be quiet, Sybille! She's nothing. You the only one who counts . . ."

So Sybille would speak with her eyes alone. He would come slowly back to his senses, half disoriented, half inebriated, enraged at having been torn away from that other planet upon which lovemaking cast him. The ground as soft as a woman's lips. There was no sky or sea in that place. Only the earth, out into infinity, scattered with female bodies transformed into rocks or else trees. He would climb up a tree, lay down on a rock. He would press his lips to the wood, to the stone, and breathe hard until he felt a shudder of life. The tree or the stone would come to life, breathe, become a woman's body. He would triumph over death.

Like a god in that other land, Gino had already observed numerous metamorphoses, when the girl at his side would form a heart with her mouth to evoke love and marriage. Inane ideas that would immediately land him back in his bed in Point-à-Pitre, where his innumerable conquests lazed. He would hang on to indigo foliage, to branches with red stems. His fingers would dig into the ground, trying to bring back a bit of earth from the blessed land. Sadly, his empty fists would always open on to the mystery of his life lines. Big *M*'s in capital letters marked on both palms. The *M* of his marriage predicted by a second cousin, an apprentice fortune teller. If he sniffed his hands, ardently searching for the smell of leaves, he would only find the natural and artificial odors of real women. Cheap perfumes, adulterated Eau de Cologne mixed with love potions, musk that had been tampered with, rum and alcohol. Milk, blood, and sweat.

He saw her as slimy and servile. But Sybille was blind. She would kiss him over and over, clinging to him pitifully. He would push her aside. Jump out of bed . . . "Oh! You got to go! Get dressed! They going to worry about you at your place! Get going!"

In Gino's eyes, she was no different than the others. She begged for sweet words, one last kiss, a caress, a token of his fidelity, a gold ring . . . But he wasn't listening to her anymore. He was shaking out the sheets furiously, his face suddenly closed, in a hurry to erase the imprint of their close quarter combat from the bed.

"Good Lord, Sisi! What have you done? What will become of you? My poor Sisi! How are we going to tell Judes that you expecting a baby? Oh, why did you follow that long-faced nigger?" moaned Coraline.

"We're going to be married. He's committed himself."

"Nigger's promise!"

Hand on his heart, Gino swore more than once to keep his word. He was simply waiting to inform his mother, a woman of fragile health, whom he needed to handle gently and help her to accept the idea of losing her only son. A month went by in hope of a marriage proposal. The silence Judes had locked himself into and Coraline's wailing, combined with prayers exhorting the saints to watch over Sybille and condemn Gino to the flames of hell.

One day, feeling backed into a corner, he stopped her in a hallway in the hospital. Bad news . . . His mother's illness had grown worse. He was taking all his savings out of the bank. Buying a plane ticket for France where a well-known professor was going to operate on the poor woman. The ceremony had to be put off. So, if she wanted to wear a white dress at the church, with a crown of orange blossoms, Gino had thought about a charitable woman. She, a neighbor with expertise, would accept to provoke a miscarriage for a reasonable price. She knew how to hold her tongue. Afterward . . . afterward, when his mother was on the road to recovery. Afterward, he'd see about marrying her and giving her children . . .

Sybille took a step backward. She immediately straightened up as if she'd been stuffed into her mother Noémie's corset of pride.

Marcello! She thought of her dead little brother in the same instant . . .

"Marcello! You promised, Gino . . ."

"It's not my fault, Sybille! I have to take care of my mama!"

"You remember, Gino? Tell me you remember . . . You agreed we would name him Marcello . . . You sang, Marcello o-o, life you will come to know ow-ow! Do you remember Gino?"

He grew angry, "It's not my fault! My mother is very sick! I don't have the money to marry you! If you can't understand that, let's just forget about it!"

"It's Marie, Gino! You prefer Marie?" Sybille sobbed.

He laughed.

"Of course I do! The two of you are like night and day. You pathetic, girl, a pathetic nutcase . . . Marie don't ask for nothing. She just spreads her legs and gets on with it!"

He left her with those words. A pirouette and adieu Sybille! Adieu wedding and family!

"Lied! *Mentè*!" cried Coraline. "He never wanted you to have his name. He took you for a ride, and you ain't the first one . . ."

For a time, Gino's last words ran riot in Sybille's mind, like weeds in an abandoned garden. Sybille thought she would go mad . . . Easily follow the trail that her mama Noémie had blazed. Eat earth. Plunge into her own certitudes as if into fecund waters, catch stars by the thousands, fish by the basketful, truths anchored in the far corners of her heart. And then believe that no one ever died. And walk proud and dignified without really understanding why . . . Proud and dignified in an imaginary corset.

But if at times she stood up straight like Noémie, driven from behind by the winds of dementia, most often Sybille wandered the streets of Pointe-à-Pitre broken and harried. Sunk in silence, moving with the steps of a sleepwalker, hiding-binding her belly in cloths tied fast, head clouded with pipe dreams.

Thanks to Coraline's miraculous prayers, Sybille showed up at the nursing school examination, in spite of everything. She recited her lesson on tuberculosis, went through the practical part of the test like an automat, and succeeded in obtaining her diploma.

She ran into Marie on several occasions. La Jalousie would

suddenly appear, as if having sprung out of some corner, upon turning into a street, in front of a market stall. Always the same lies.

"Oh, I swear to it! Oh! Oh! It's true . . . Only once, one sole time, I only went with Gino one little time! And I wanted to ask your forgiveness a hundred times, Sisi! A hundred times, I swear to it! He came looking for me!"

Sybille listened to Marie, watched her sly lips flapping, felt as if she were being clawed at each confession. She remembered her at the age of six, sitting quietly on the bench at school in Grand-Saut. And then at eight, her mouth in the shape of an O, lying on the bed next to her, miming the gestures of the famous lovers. Horrid Marie, nicknamed La Jalousie because one day she'd wept in rage at seeing a young married couple kissing in front of the steps to the church. After that it wasn't long before she started lending her body to the boys who took her out of curiosity, to suck on her little mint-flavored *coucoune,* but didn't go back twice. As soon as they'd had their fill, overcome with mistrust and disgust, they made a run for it. The girls detested her and were offended by her presence at Sybille's side, imposing her friendship with suave authority. Fascinating Marie, who, under the white voiles of a sister of the Church of Saint-Simoleon, dissimulated an ardent body, always prepared to succumb to the temptations of the flesh.

When, at the age of nine, Sybille had left Saint-Simoleon, feelings of sadness and relief grappled with one another in her heart. Marie hadn't cried. She had hugged her and given her a sour kiss. And then, swearing she would love her till the end of time, she'd extorted from her the pledge to continue playing the last act of the lovers from Basse-Terre.

Twelve years later, having recently passed her nursing examination and preparing to go into exile in France, Sybille was no longer so gullible. When she found herself face to face with Marie in a side street in Point-à-Pitre, she was careful not to say anything about expecting Gino's child.

But the other girl, who must have had a good laugh about it with Gino, already knew everything.

"So, have a nice trip, my little Sisi! And take care of that little bird sleeping in your belly!" she advised in the stead of a good-bye, with that placid face and that smooth look, those black lips of hers.

Sybille had shivered in the cold wind blowing from Marie. She promised herself to never again allow her to come near as long as she lived. To flee just as old Suzanne had told her to. Disappear. Go far away to escape Marie, Gino, Clothilde, Robert, and Noémie . . . Go away so as to stop feeling the hoarse breath of the dead on the back of her neck and the sulfurous halo of madness. Go away to save Marcello . . .

In Paris, Sybille observed herself closely, her slightest acts and words, for fear of detecting the illness that had afflicted Noémie at work. Fear of forgetting that people were mortal. Fear of awaiting the deceased, of conversing with them as if they were alive. Fear of walking straight, proud, and dignified without really knowing why, arms dangling, mind blank. Fear of seeing herself eat dirt. Of becoming rabid over a piece of blood sausage. Fear of not recognizing herself in the mirror. Face deformed, mouth turned into a long beak. Fear of babbling to herself in the street. Fear of giving birth to a dead child.

She'd immediately found a position in a private clinic, in the vicinity of Neuilly. A place to stay in a small attic room in a building in the tenth arrondissement of Paris. Every week she'd written to Coraline, who was tormented by the fact she was alone and easy prey to the innumerable demons in Paris.

But Sybille didn't feel lonely. She had her belly that she carried high, walked proudly with down the halls of the clinic and the streets of Paris. Her belly without a papa that was her treasure and constantly reminded her of Noémie.

The illness had come over Noémie before her craving for blood sausage, before the death of Robert in the room with Clothilde in Basse-Terre, before that of her little boy. She would shoot strange looks at people sometimes. Slip into silences when an answer was expected. Ask out-of-place questions and rattle off irrational comments that Robert never reacted to, as if he didn't rely on reason himself. She would take Sybille off on long walks during which walking fast was the only destination. Walk along without exchanging a word with the wind whipping her face, eyes gazing out beyond the horizon. Walk along with her hand curled in Noémie's cold rough palm. Watch her mama shoo away invisible shapes flitting about in front of her, cock her ear to faceless voices, tear up new clothes, roll around on the ground.

They had followed the remains of Robert and Marcello together in stride. One was large with a light oak finish and one small, off-white, the size of a shoe box. Nitila, Marie's mother, had chanted her couplet about life and death. But Robert and Marcello had not been resuscitated for all that. The caskets had remained closed. And the myriads of prayers for children that had been haunting Sybille's mind had changed nothing. Death was still death, and life that diabolical net in which humans circled, like the fish her papa Robert used to bring in from the ocean depths, until they lost their breath.

In the old days, Sybille would laugh as she watched the fish dancing in the fishermen's skiffs. They were jumping around between life and death. She waited, amused, for the very last jerk, the ultimate shudder. And when life had gone out of them all together, she would take them by the tail and jab her finger into their bulging eyes and their puffed out bellies.

The earth had closed back over the two coffins as the Christians pressed around Noémie, repeating Nitila's words of hope . . .

"Rejoice! Do not cry! For you see, child, death is life and life is death!"

"Sincere condolences . . ."

"Saint Cere Cordon Lantz!

"Saint Lantz!"

"Saint Lantz! Give my little brother Marcello back to me!"

Sybille found herself alone with Noémie. The suddenly immense cabin echoed from all corners with the growing madness of her mother who was opening the door to the ghosts. The ghosts of her papa Robert and of her little brother Marcello whom Noémie gave her breast to and watched growing bigger and heavier.

They spent two years together. Sybille would sometimes hold her mama's hand, battling for it against that other world filled with voices and dearly regretted faces.

Two years shared between Marie and Noémie, Robert and Marcello before Judes and Coraline took her into their home in Point-à-Pitre.

Sybille had always thought she would give birth to a boy. Throughout her pregnancy, she dreamt about her little brother. Had pictured him again, hanging head down from the umbilical cord between Noémie's spread legs. Poor little body, all blue, skin already wrinkled, hair sticky. Poor little Marcello . . .

He was barely one year old when she'd knocked at the door of the owner of the building on rue Danton. A certain Madame Montrevault, "an eccentric," people said. She owned a fine apartment right over her own that she had never rented.

"Try your luck, who knows?" a nurse had said to her lightly. "The woman has her humors. Maybe you'll happen to find her in a good one and she'll take pity on you . . ."

14

In the inner courtyard, surrounded by the blind walls of the neighboring buildings, there were three ficus, two stone benches, a fountain, and perches. The birds searched for their doubles in small dangling mirrors. Preened their feathers. Flew from the trees to the wall where the missing bricks had been replaced with nests. Swallows pecked around in saucers filled with sugar, with grains of brown rice.

"It's because of this courtyard and its birds that my father moved The Kreyol. Before, it was an antique shop owned by an old Jewish lady. When she died, they put the shop up for sale along with all its doo-dads. They weren't valuable objects, but personal items people had gotten rid of, that she'd bought for a dollar or found on the street, fished out of attics . . . You know, combs and brushes, how do you say . . . chipped cups . . . portraits of strangers, yellow-yellowed doilies . . . cupboards with no doors, stained mirrors, dressing tables, tables and chairs that needed mending or varnishing . . ." James-Lee laughed. "Ah, all these stories bore you, don't they? And my French is very imperfect, isn't it?"

I implored him to continue his story. I assured him his French was excellent and even asked him who had taught it to him. He answered that it was Henry, in remembrance of his mother and out of love for France.

I was in a strange frame of mind listening to those stories of birds and baubles without being able to concentrate on what he was saying. More than anything else, I was trying to capture his attention, to tell him with my eyes that I wanted to feel his hands on my skin. Just that. But he turned his eyes away, lost in another era, as if he could see the Jewish woman in the midst of her old things. He had a slight accent. He spoke slowly, placing one word carefully after the other. His voice vibrated a little, found its way into secret places in my body. I let myself be swept away on the intonations that were whispering so sweetly inside of me, like a pleasant little breeze, a very deep caress, the wave that comes endlessly back to smooth the ripples of sand on the beach.

"Oh, you know, in the middle of summer there are even more birds here! And my father is happy. People are always surprised and you should hear the things they say. They claim it's a Garden of Eden in the heart of New York. We don't know anything about these birds. They arrive and settle in as if it were their home. They eat, drink, sing. And they're free. It dates back to the time of the old lady. No one can explain how she lured them here. Perhaps . . . with sugar alone."

Lila and I had been in the United States almost a week, going from the restaurant to the hotel where Henry had reserved rooms for us. Neither of us felt the desire to visit New York, its avenues, its museums, the lights of Broadway. Lila wanted to piece the past back together with Henry and James-Lee. And I went along with her to see James-Lee, who, in the wake of Marcello, had suddenly become my sunshine.

A beautiful sun thrown up into my sky at the noon hour of my life that didn't even cast a shadow on the ground I walked lightly over, airborne, relieved of my burdens.

I learned, without being truly astonished, that James-Lee was Lila's son, her only child whom she had let go because of his color and because of the era too and of "what will people say." Her boy, whom she'd never been able to forget and whom I'd given back to her when I'd arrived in her life with my little Marcello in my arms. Her child, lost and found, then flown off again, the day Marcello got on the plane for Guadeloupe. No,

I hadn't really taken into account the silences she must have had to keep over all those years when, like two mothers, we'd cherished Marcello with all our hearts and all of our heartaches. My Marcello, upon whom she'd lavished the tenderness that had been destined for James-Lee. My son whom she had loved in order to repent for having abandoned James-Lee to Henry as soon as he was born, for having driven him out of her life.

I didn't have time to judge her. For that matter, no one even tried to explain it to me. That was just the way it was, that's all. James-Lee was Lila's son. It was evident. They talked a little. Seemed to appreciate one another. Didn't really make other overtures . . . I was the most excited of everyone. I had received James-Lee from Lila like a living gift, the man she'd drawn out of her past so that I would understand, at least once in my life, the meaning of the word *love*.

I wasn't bitter about Gino anymore. Not even tormented by Marie La Jalousie. Not even worried about Marcello. I was in New York, in a courtyard whose only purpose was for the babbling, the well-being, and the reveling of birds.

I was no longer pained by the thought of my poor mama Noémie . . . Not even obsessed with the mystery of my papa Robert dead in the arms of that girl Clothilde, the queen of flowers in Basse-Terre. Not even haunted by the vision of my little brother Marcello, all blue, hanging by his umbilical cord between Noémie's legs. I was in New York, new, smooth, buoyed up by the voice of James-Lee, who was telling me stories about birds.

I was nothing more than a beating heart, starved for love. Nothing but a body, voracious for the body of James-Lee. And I couldn't find the words to tell him. Only had my eyes to let him know. And I had no other choice but to let my hand linger, forgetfully leave it on his. Let my body speak, like Gina Lollobrigida or Sophia Loren. Cross and uncross my legs until he got dizzy. Walk around in plunging necklines, short tight-fitting dresses. And to explain the reason for that behavior, stammer about having never suffered so much from the heat. It was so hot in New York!

James-Lee had been married. Ten years. In the seventies, eighties. One of his children lived with its mother, south of Atlanta. He never spoke about his marriage. From time to time, his daughter, Helen, a lawyer like her Aunt Sundra, was able to get free from their office in Harlem and join us at The Kreyol. "Always at dinner time!" Henry exclaimed. As for Rodgers, Henry's third son, they'd only seen him once: a visit paid out of pure curiosity. To verify at last that James-Lee's mother was real. That incredible Lila who had been a ghost, a shadow walking in Lana's footsteps throughout their childhood. Lana whom they all called mom, even James-Lee, just like his sister and brothers, though he knew he had another one, back there in Paris, France. A Lila, a little flower, whom he sometimes dreamt about while touching the French woman's smile. A black and white face on the thick glossy paper of a photograph dating back to the forties. Dark curls. Light, dreamy eyes . . . Lila who didn't resemble the broken woman who'd been introduced to him as his mother, almost fifty years later. The little flower he didn't recognize in that old porcelain doll with too much makeup on. Blonde mama under her gray hair in need of a new dye-job. Unexpected mama, so close and yet always so far away at the same time, kept at a distance through tactful silence.

Leaning on their elbows at a table in the restaurant, Lila and Henry had once again gone back to their youth that they were feverishly painting, day after day, each in his own fashion. Memories that seemed to have different colors in the other's eyes. Bright colors and wide shapeless brushstrokes for Lila. Pastels and fine lines for Henry who depicted the faces of the past with incredible accuracy.

"Little Flower! Do you remember . . ." faltered Henry.

"Tatata!" cried Lila. "No more little flower or bouquet of lilacs! Stop telling those tales of yours. I told you I didn't want to get married, you remember? But that's all you could think about!"

"Forever!' he murmured, a bit dreamily, head thrown back. "Forever, Lila . . ."

•••

When she heard the door slam behind the abortionist, Lila truly hoped that Henry's child had left her body. She closed her eyes so she wouldn't see the little egg transpierced, its soul torn in two. Thinking of Henry who'd been asking her to marry him constantly, she'd cried with the tears of an abandoned woman. 1946, a dark year, she sighed.

Henry never believed that abortion story. She'd thrown that horror story about knitting needles skillfully wielded by the abortionist in his face. She'd talked about the problems that the birth of a child of mixed race would cause in that world in which blacks and whites had always hated one another. She'd laughed and sobbed at the same time and had slapped him so he would come back down to reality. As an excuse, she'd used the disappointment of her parent's from Sarthe, who, according to her, would have never accepted to reach out to a black son-in-law. Would have never taken into their arms that café au lait child that she would have been ashamed to admit had been born of her flesh. But Henry didn't come down from his clouds.

She'd called him a nigger. Dirty Negro! Jigaboo! He shook his head, pulled her over to him. Lay her down against his chest. Put his ear up to Lila's belly. Tried to hear the little heart that, according to him, was beating like a drum through the nocturnal sounds. Drum from the hills of Saint John that took him back to Hamilton's Gardens, promised hope for black folk. Just like back in the days when Nanny and Percy killed themselves. Drum beating in rage and pain. Wild sound of the drum that the trade winds wafted from heart to heart, soul to soul, cabin to cabin, announcing Percy's hanging and Nanny's poisoning. Little heart that was galloping along like the horse Columbus, ridden by Michael over the roads of Saint John. Poor Michael! Poor Michael . . . Ever faster, spurred on by the wind of anger and humiliation. Ever faster, to stop thinking about Jenny in the arms of Master George. The man who had crushed his dreams and pulverized the prayers he thought had been answered the day of his engagement to Jenny. His lovely Jenny. Poor Michael! Poor Michael! Ancient drum upon which the worn fingers of the *tanbouyé*-drummer were smashing his human dignity. Poor Michael!

In vain, Lila awaited the blood predicted by the abortionist. The blood that would deliver her from Henry's dreams and phantoms. When her belly was bloated, she wouldn't go out of her room anymore. As if she were going to give birth to some monstrous creature.

"Nigger! Dirty Negro! I hope you're happy!" she screamed. "You got what you wanted, eh? Well I don't want this brat! You can keep it for yourself . . . And as soon as it's over, you get out of my life! I don't ever want to see you again, you hear? You get out, you and your kid! Go on, scram!"

Henry would listen to her; he understood perfectly well that the dreadful words tumbling from Lila's lips were simply filled with her own distress. Sometimes she talked to herself loudly and forcefully, so that he would hear her and be wounded by her words. She spoke of Hans and the Jewish people who'd probably been arrested because of him, her German lover. She swore she would have done better to carry the child of one of Hitler's soldiers than to have a black man get her pregnant.

Henry contemplated her, looking like a whipped dog. He was suddenly knocked back into his teenage body, furious with his father George MacDowell and his mama Jenny. Filled with horror at the idea of that white father who had popped up on the day of Auntie Peggy's funeral. He thought of his companion in arms, Isidor Deblavieux, dead before having been able to ask his mama Nini to pardon him. Pardon and thank you . . . And Henry felt nothing but compassion for Lila whom he believed was shaken and terrorized by the life that was growing inside of her.

He helped her, consoled by the certainty that Lila would see things differently one day, in a year, ten years, fifty years. And while she showered insults on him, he washed her clothes, cleaned the apartment, and prepared all the meals that she would push away in disgust. Delicious dishes that he invented as he hummed songs from his island.

• • •

"Do you remember, Lila? You didn't want to swallow a bite."

"I didn't want to eat? Yes I did! I ate! Everything you cooked."

"You've forgotten again, Lila," Henry smiled.

"Go ahead, dare to say I'm crazy!"

"No! You didn't eat, Little Flower."

"I pecked at my food like a little bird, that's all! If not, our James-Lee wouldn't have survived. Use your brain!"

Henry knit his brow, ran a hand through his graying hair. His eyes were searching the past. Fifty years ago, that was quite some time to go back, colors to freshen up, moments to put end to end. Fifty years of hoping she would finally find peace within herself.

"The day you gave birth, you were . . ."

"Oh no! Please, Henry, spare me that! Let's talk about your leaving with James-Lee again instead!" cut in Lila.

Henry excused himself for a minute and, like every evening at the same time, disappeared into the kitchen to taste the sauces and congratulate the cooks who were hurriedly preparing the last dishes. He came back with a glass of chilled soy milk, which he set down in front of Lila.

"We didn't leave," he continued. "You threw us out. Our love affair was over. You were horrified at having a black child. So, off to America!"

"Tatata! You must admit you didn't really insist!"

"You weren't speaking to me, Lila! You were angry! You were ashamed, weren't you . . ."

Lila shrugged her shoulders. "You ran off too fast, like a thief. You stranded me. You didn't give me enough time. You left me alone with my regrets. And when you disappeared, the Jews came back . . ."

"They still there?" asked Henry. "They never let go of you?"

"On the building across the street . . . the women, the men, and the children, the trains and the buses . . ."

Time was slipping by. Sticky and sluggish, I followed James-Lee in his comings and goings. Love is really something . . . The shadow of your shadow, the shadow of your dog, the shadow of your hand, as Lila used to sing so well. James-Lee seemed to be getting used to my more than pressing presence. He still grew ecstatic over the mystery of the birds at The Kreyol and that of the old antique dealer. But he also talked about Lana, the woman who had brought him up, his father, his sister, and his brothers Rodgers and Michael. He had at last started talking about himself. Which fascinated me. He'd cried when Lana died. Being quite frank, he admitted that he wasn't sure he would shed a single tear when Lila died. He confided to me that Lana had given him just as much love as she had Sundra, Rodgers, and Michael. When she began making those cushions with pom-poms smaller and smaller, he prayed every night that she wouldn't leave this life. He'd held her hand and watched her die.

His eyes always grew moist when he said my mom Lana. He spoke about his daughter, Helen, and his marriage that had turned out to be a disaster. And then three days before our departure, James-Lee invited me out to dinner at a restaurant in the middle of Chinatown.

"Go, my little Billy! He's all yours!" Lila had called out to her, with a sparkle in her eye. "Get yourself nice and spruced up and never forget that nothing in this world can beat love."

I'd picked out a tight-fitting dress, bought for three dollars on Broadway. "Three dollars, sure isn't a high price to pay for love!" the salesgirl from Port-au-Prince had insisted. We exchanged a few words in Creole, which, ringing out oddly such a long way from home, brought us together. She claimed I looked like Whitney Houston, that I was beautiful in my cheap dress.

"*Fout ou bèl négres! Fout ou bèl!* You damned pretty, Negress! You damned pretty!"

And those flattering words had remained with me all the way back to the hotel. Gentle words murmured to me by a woman, just like myself, who was awaiting love and dreaming of America in Creole.

That evening, for the first time, James-Lee held my gaze. And he proved to be curious. Wanted to know what role I played in Lila's life, his father Henry's beloved wilted flower. In a whisper, I told him the story of my parents, Robert and Noémie. As if it were a folktale, I related the life of Clothilde, the dream harvester, flower gatherer, and femme fatale. I recited Nitila's words, "Life is death and death is life." I denounced Marie La Jalousie's traps, Gino's lies. I told him of Marcello's birth. And then, we shared our bird stories. The birds that twittered and sang, died only to be resuscitated here and there, from cabin to cage, from island to island. Eternally . . . All over the world. And as I was telling him about the destiny of Néhémie, seized with regret on her deathbed for having missed out on love, and the enigma of the rosebud in the bird's beak, he sought out my hand.

Suddenly my heart felt as if everything were light as a feather. In the soft light of the suspended lamps and candleholders in the Chinese restaurant, the gilt dragons were breathing flames. Wings spread on the walls, awaiting new skies, they believed they were alive. All they needed was life's breath to awaken their bodies and let them take flight. They were like humans who lacked only breath.

When James-Lee took me back to the hotel that night, he asked me if I liked New York, if I was a Parisian like Lila, forever haunted by my phantoms. I answered that the ones that lived within me were like the birds in our legends. To house their tormented souls, they travelled from body to body. James-Lee smiled gently.

15

That October it was rainy in Paris. In the tree branches, the leaves were still hesitating between red and green. It was mild. The open window let in the din of honking horns. New York was far away, but since we'd come back, Lila had found a means of mentioning it every day.

"Did you see, Billy? Nothing!!! Not a single reproach . . . After all these years, he could have been embittered. He hasn't changed in the least. Except his vegetarian thing . . . And my son! He's handsome, isn't he? The two of you, I'm jealous of your youth. Eh? See how great love is, Billy? What'd I tell you? Oh, if only I were twenty years younger, Billy!"

Lila had already had two heart attacks. Her doctor came to see her in the evenings. I avoided upsetting her. I jumped as soon as she raised a finger. I strained my neck out on the balcony to see the shadows of her past. We thought about Marcello who telephoned us fairly often. But most of all about Henry and James-Lee's America.

We were constantly trying to remember the smell of the dishes, the hubbub of the streets, the honking of the yellow cabs that drove past in front of The Kreyol. We listened to *So Near, So Far, Musings for Miles* by Joe Henderson, which James-Lee had given me at the airport. We promised ourselves to go back as soon as possible. In December. Because Henry had decreed that every human being should experience Christmas in New York at least once in his lifetime, Lila had acquiesced.

After America, we just wanted to rub each other with gentle words, warm our hearts, and not move around too much for fear of bursting the bubble that Henry and James-Lee's America had closed us up in.

Up to the very end, we thought she'd have enough energy to go back to New York. I'd already picked up our tickets. We were supposed to take off on December 20. Lila left us on the fifteenth.

She was lying stiff on the carpet. I immediately thought of Henry, of James-Lee, and of Marcello. The haste to share the misfortune . . . Not stay alone with death. It was nine o'clock in the morning in Paris and four o'clock in Guadeloupe.

Judes and Coraline were both over eighty years old. They considered the telephone a barbaric instrument that might startle them at any moment. They only used it themselves on rare occasions to talk with the home healthcare nurse: she was an old maid from the old school who still boiled her needles and syringes in a kitchen pot. She came once a week to take Coraline's blood pressure.

There were six long rings. Then Judes picked up the receiver. His worn, quavering voice sent a pang to my heart, and I swore to myself I would go back to Guadeloupe very soon. In the background, Coraline was begging him to tell her everything. As soon as he spoke my name, she started whining and letting out little cries . . . "Oh, what? Our little Sisi has run into trouble. My God! No! Tell me, Judo! Oh, my God!"

"Oh, my God! Dear Lord!" just like back in the days when she used to talk in a low voice about my mother's troubles and the tragedy in Basse-Terre . . .

"Oh, my God! Dear Lord!" When I would come home from school with bloody knees.

"Oh, my God!" The day I obtained my diploma . . . The first time she'd glared at Gino, whom she felt was too black for me . . . And the evening I had gone to La Renaissance to see a karate film and she waited up for me, sitting in the dark. "Oh my God! What you up to with that mean nigger of ill-repute, Sisi?"

When I could hear Coraline better, her expressions, so close, so very old and infantile at the same time, it brought her entirely back to me; I felt the need to feel someone's arms around me. The arms of a mother . . . Noémie, Coraline, or Lila. Of a man, those of James-Lee that wrapped around me so well in New York.

"Oh, my God! Dear Lord! What's going on, Sisi?"

I lied straight away, "Nothing! Everything's fine!" And then I begged their pardon for the late hour and the fear I'd caused them. I hadn't prepared the words to announce Lila's death. So I blurted out that I missed them. That I needed to hear their voices. Know how Marcello was acting. Coraline whispered that he wasn't very talkative, didn't understand Creole very well. Above all, he wanted to get to know Guadeloupe and his family on Gino's side. He read the phone directory as if it were a novel and wrote down the numbers of everyone listed who bore the same name. He went to high school regularly . . . "You could have at least brought him here once . . . After all these years . . . Oh, my God! Dear Lord! I'm not blaming you, Sisi."

I marked a pause.

But she went on, "Come on, don't worry! This is Marcello's home. His youth is a blessing . . . And you did a good job with his upbringing. He sleeping right now. Should I wake him? I'll tell him you called tomorrow . . . And when you coming?"

I promised—as I always did—smiled into the telephone, buttered them up, and sent them kisses as I watched Lila's motionless, already graying face . . . Her closed eyes, her hardly mussed hair, and her lipstick that looked as if it were freshly applied, as if she had made herself up for a date. She'd fallen in front of her armchair. And I hadn't even thought to lay her in her bed. I'd only thought about the men in her life . . . Marcello, Henry, and James-Lee. I would have liked to hear them cry out, "Oh no! Not Lila already! It's just not fair! What? What time was it?" Useless words to relieve my grief.

Marcello called Sybille back four days after Lila's funeral. He cried as soon as she told him the news. Of course he regretted not having put his arms around Lila the day he'd left for Guadeloupe, nine months earlier. He felt bad about having avoided her kisses. Having felt ashamed when she walked beside him.

Sybille consoled him, assuring him that life really was the way Lila had described it: cluttered with trunks filled with "I should have's," with shattered vials, with chains and keys.

Holding back the sobs in his throat, Marcello declared that he loved her with all his heart.

"Oh yes, I love you, my little mama. And I'll never forget Lila . . . Did she suffer terribly, Mama?"

"No, Marcello. She didn't wake up, that's all."

"What do you mean?"

"Well, she left in her sleep. Her soul took flight during the night . . ."

"Really? She was sleeping?" there was a note of surprise in Marcello's voice, as if he felt that that particular way of dying corresponded exactly to Lila's image, to what she had stood for all her life.

Feeling his pain was subsiding, Sybille went on in a lighter tone of voice, "Now tell me about yourself, Lolo . . ."

"Well, I might go and live with my father. I feel like being with my brothers and sisters."

"How many are there, Lolo?"

"There are five of us . . . We get along well . . ."

"I'm happy for you, Lolo."

"My father is proud of me."

"I'm proud of you too, Lolo."

"So when are you leaving for New York?"

"Tomorrow."

"Wouldn't you rather come to Guadeloupe?"

"Yes, of course . . . But Lila and I had already planned this trip. I have to go and join them over there. But I'll come and see you soon with James-Lee . . . Okay? Let's say goodbye for now, all right?"

They hung up sending each other kisses.

Sybille sat down on the bed, laid the portrait of Lila in her suitcase, which she closed gently. Outside, night had fallen and the ponderous sky glittered with thousands of stars that she would have liked to just sit there counting until the first glimmers of dawn. Stay up thinking about her love, James-Lee, who just might know how to find that taste of eternity.